"I wouldn't choose a different path..."

Adel's voice was quiet. "It's more fulfilling than I ever dreamed to be a part of things this way. I don't want to take on another husband or his children. You're right. I don't want it. I want to see what *Gott* has on this path He set me on."

"Maybe you'll end up being Redemption's official matchmaker," Jake said.

"Maybe. But I'm not a snob."

"You're not a snob," he said quietly. "I'm sorry I said it."

"Thank you."

"But this isn't going to be a one-way street, either," he said with a smile touching his lips. "You'll be digging into my life, but I'm going to figure you out, too, Adel."

Adel rolled her eyes. "You can try, but we're better off keeping to our mission."

The grin he shot her suggested that he'd just accepted a challenge, and somehow she doubted it was only about finding his wife.

Were all bachelors this difficult?

If her goal was to become the matchmaker around here, she might be taking on more trouble than she ever imagined...

Patricia Johns is a *Publishers Weekly* bestselling author who writes from Alberta, Canada. She has her Hon. BA in English literature and currently writes for Harlequin's Love Inspired and Heartwarming lines. She also writes Amish romance for Kensington Books. You can find her at patriciajohns.com.

Books by Patricia Johns

Love Inspired

Redemption's Amish Legacies

Montana Twins

Harlequin Heartwarming

Amish Country Haven

Visit the Author Profile page at LoveInspired.com for more titles.

The Amish Matchmaker's Choice

Patricia Johns

LOVE INSPIRED
INSPIRATIONAL ROMANCE

LOVE INSPIRED®
INSPIRATIONAL ROMANCE

Recycling programs for this product may not exist in your area.

ISBN-13: 978-1-335-56772-7

The Amish Matchmaker's Choice

Love Inspired
22 Adelaide St. West, 41st Floor
Toronto, Ontario M5H 4E3, Canada
www.LoveInspired.com

Printed in U.S.A.

I have taught thee in the way of wisdom;
I have led thee in right paths.
—*Proverbs* 4:11

To my husband and our son.
Thank you for your support as I write.
I love you both more than anything!

Chapter One

Jake Knussli sat on the couch next to Bishop Glick, his palms damp. The windows were cranked open, letting in a whisper of breeze, and Jake adjusted his suspenders over his shoulders. It wasn't just the hot July day that brought sweat to his brow. The bishop had an ulterior motive to suggesting the Draschel Bed and Breakfast for him to stay in while his uncle's farmhouse was fumigated.

"So you need a wife," Adel Draschel said. She looked as cool and neat as a spring day, and she regarded him with a distanced, thoughtful expression as if he were some unknown entity instead of someone she'd grown up with.

Adel was exactly his age, thirty-seven—they'd gone to school together in that one-room schoolhouse as *kinner*. The years had been kinder to her than they had been to him, he thought. With her soft figure and creamy skin, set off by auburn hair, tucked under a silky white *kapp*. There were a few lines around her eyes, but she looked more youthful than he did with the gray working its way into the stubble on his chin. Adel bent over a tray, pouring tea, one finger on the teapot's lid to keep it in place.

"*Yah*, I do need a wife," Jake replied.

"If Jacob is going to inherit that farm, then we have to find someone quickly," Bishop Glick added, stroking his wiry salt-and-pepper beard with one hand.

"You mentioned it was rushed," Adel said, passing a teacup to the bishop. "Why now? He's been back for a few months now."

"I needed to come back properly," Jake said. "I had other things to worry about, like getting baptized."

"How much time do we have now before the will runs out?" she asked.

"Two weeks," the bishop replied.

Adel blew out a breath. "Two weeks!"

She turned that skeptical stare back onto Jake, and he suppressed the urge to squirm. He wasn't asking *her* to marry him. The bishop thought she could act as matchmaker. Granted, it was a short period of time to secure a marriage match, but she didn't need to look at him like it was quite that impossible, either.

Jake fiddled with one side of his suspenders across his shoulder where his shirt was getting damp from sweat. He was still wearing his straw hat, and he pulled it off his head and scrubbed a hand through his hair, which was still growing out that last bit from an *Englisher* style.

"What did the will say exactly?" Adel asked, politely and rather pointedly ignoring his attempt to smooth out his appearance.

"It said that if I was to inherit the family farm from Uncle Johannes," Jake said, dropping his hat onto his knee, "then I needed to be both Amish again and married within six months of his death."

"But why did Johannes do that?" she asked, shaking her head. "Do we know? He didn't have any *kinner* of his own, and Jake, you are the logical one to inherit that land. I can understand asking that you be Amish again to inherit, but married, too? Why make it difficult?"

Jake exchanged a look with the bishop. He

and Bishop Glick had discussed this for a couple of hours the night before. Why would Johannes have made those stipulations in his will? Because it felt like his uncle was being obstinate, even in death.

"I think he wanted to bring Jacob home," Bishop Glick said. "And a home grows roots with marriage. I didn't know the specifics of his will until after his death, but I did pray with him before his passing. Johannes knew his time was close, and he wanted to be right with *Gott*. He spoke about wanting to make up for past wrongs. Maybe this was an attempt to do just that."

"If he wanted to make up for some wrongs, this setup seems to be creating a few new ones," Adel said, and Jake smiled in response to her wry perspective.

The bishop took a sip of his tea but didn't say anything.

"So if you aren't legally married in two weeks, then what happens to the land?" Adel asked.

"It goes to my cousin Alphie," Jake replied.

Adel leaned back in her chair, then she turned to the bishop. "And if we don't find anyone for him to marry? What then?"

"Jacob?" the bishop said, turning toward him.

What choice would Jake have? He'd been quietly looking around ever since he returned, hoping to find someone the natural way, but it was harder than he thought. If his cousin Alphie was very kind, he might let Jake run the farm with him, since it would go to him if Jake's quest to find a wife by the will's deadline failed. But it would only ever be a job, not his own property in that case. Their family dynamic had been a difficult one—nowhere near the Amish ideals.

"If we can't find me a wife, then I will thank you for trying and for the time you put into it, and I will accept that *Gott* has other plans," Jake said.

Adel nodded somberly, exhaling slowly. "And what do you have to offer a wife, Jacob?"

Jake met her gaze, and he felt a smile tickling the corners of his lips.

"You're acting like I'm a stranger, Adel. I used to pull your *kapp* strings when we were *kinner*. You know me."

"I knew a boy," Adel said, her cheeks pinking. "This is a grown man in front of me. And a little tease who used to pester us girls isn't exactly going to recommend you to the marriageable women in our area."

"Point taken," he replied, sobering. "I'm a hard worker. I have a nice little nest egg in the bank, and if I'm married in time, you can add a paid-off farm to that. I'm in relatively good condition for my age, but you'd have to be judge of that."

Adel looked away, annoyance flashing in her blue eyes, but he couldn't help himself. He wasn't the stranger she was pretending he was.

"And I don't drink, smoke or gamble," he added.

"That's a relief," she replied wryly. "But for my own conscience, I need to ask a few questions. I hope you don't mind." Her gaze flickered toward the bishop.

"Go ahead," Bishop Glick said.

Just for a moment, Adel's perfect poise cracked, and he saw a flicker of the girl he used to know all those years ago—opinionated, fiery—and he felt a rush of satisfaction at finally getting through that prim-and-proper reserve of hers.

"Jacob, *why* are you back? Before, it seemed like you were ready to come home again." Her cheeks flushed slightly. "But now I find out that there is a will involved that was pushing you to it. Are you back just for the land?"

Jake smiled faintly. "You think that's the only reason I'm here?"

"Are you?" she asked.

"No, I'm not. I'd been thinking about coming home for a long time, but when my *daet* passed away, Uncle Johannes and I weren't exactly on good terms. There were hard words between us, and there was always some reason or other to put it off another year."

Alphie, who was actually a second cousin once removed, had filled him in on the continuing bitterness here at home whenever he got together with his cousin for a coffee. He'd known what was waiting for him.

"Will you stay Amish now?" she asked.

"*Yah.* I will stay living the Amish way. If I marry an Amish woman, I'm not going to leave the Amish life and I will stay on the farm I inherit, if that's what you're asking."

"That's exactly what I'm asking." She pressed her lips together and put her teacup down next to her. "If I set you up with someone, I need to be able to tell her that she can trust you to be a good and Amish husband."

"I understand," he said.

"That is a very big thing for me to tell a

woman," Adel said. "She would be taking my word that your character is marriageable within that short of a period of time. That is a lot to ask of me. She'd be well and truly married within a week upon my say-so."

"It's a big step," he said seriously. "It's a lot to ask of any woman. I do understand that."

Adel sighed. "The bishop speaks for you, and that should be enough." Somehow he got the sense that it wasn't, though. "And I won't be setting you up with anyone under twenty-five, for the record," she added, giving him a pointed look.

"I'm not looking to marry someone that young," Jake countered. "I'd much rather be with a woman closer to my own age."

"Good, because a woman any younger than that has other prospects still," Adel replied.

He felt the sting of those words. "Ouch."

"Sorry." Adel winced. "But asking someone to marry that quickly, she'd have to have good reason to be willing to take the risk. This is the rest of her life we're talking about, and I'm afraid that a very young woman wouldn't be able to fully understand what she was getting herself into. That would be…cruel."

"I have to agree with that." He met her gaze. Did she think he wanted some young eighteen-year-old? Because he didn't. "And I'm not marrying just anyone, either. I have a few requirements on my list, too. But for a chance to have the family farm again, I'm willing to try to find a match."

"Good. I'm glad you've been thinking about it," she said. "What are you looking for?"

"We have to find each other mutually attractive," he said. "Marriage is for life, and I want to wake up to a woman I find beautiful in spirit. And I want her to see something attractive in me, too."

"A good point," she said. "What else?"

"Like we agreed—no one too young, or too old, for that matter. I'd like a woman who is age appropriate for me. I'll trust your opinion with that."

"That's fair. What else?"

"She has to be real," he said.

Adel frowned.

"Authentic," he clarified. "She has to be open and comfortable."

"Okay." Adel nodded. "Anything else? Are you looking for a good cook? Does it matter if she has children?"

"Uh—" He exhaled slowly. "I think it would depend on the woman."

"Good." Adel nodded. "It's good that you're

staying here at my bed-and-breakfast, since it will make it easier for us to save time. My sister and I sleep here in the house, and the *dawdie* house is set up for our guests. You'll be very comfortable."

"I'm sure I will be," he agreed.

"I'm going to pray on this," Adel said. "And I'll do my best."

The bishop spread his hands. "The Lord works in mysterious ways, Adel. Perhaps He has something to achieve here. The Good Book does tell us that it isn't good for a man to be alone. I think that we can extrapolate that it is the same for women. I do enjoy seeing people married for that very reason. Two are stronger than one."

The bishop looked at Adel meaningfully, and her cheeks colored again. This conversation seemed to be expressly between the two of them. Obviously, it was a subject that had come up before.

"I have my sister here, Bishop," she said with a good-humored smile. "I'm not alone, and I have no interest in getting married again. I haven't changed my mind."

"Of course." The older man pushed himself back to his feet. "Call me sentimental, but I keep on trying to find you a match, Adel. I'll consider myself a success when I finally do. Well, I will leave you to get your guest settled in. Thank you for helping, Adel. I trust your insight."

Adel nodded. "As Mark used to say, some things take a man's leadership, and others take a woman's intuition."

"He was a wise man." The bishop and Adel both nodded soberly. Then the bishop headed for the door. "Jacob, I will leave you to Adel's care. Let's see what *Gott* provides. I'll be praying, too."

Everyone would be praying, it seemed, including Jake. While the main concern seemed to be for the poor woman who was stuck with him, Jake had the most at stake here. And they'd need all the blessing and guidance they could get. Jake rose to his feet and went to the door to grab his duffel bag that he'd left on the porch, waving to Bishop Glick as he headed back out to his buggy.

Then he turned back to Adel, who was still eyeing him with an uncertain look on her face, her cup of tea balanced on a saucer in front of her.

"Now that it's just the two of us, you can be brutally honest with me," he said. "What are my chances of finding a wife?"

"I have a few ideas." A smile lifted the corners of her lips. "We'll see what we can do."

Adel heard the sound of the bishop's buggy rolling back down the drive. Bishop Glick had been a good, personal friend of her late husband's. The two men had discussed various community issues together, late into the night, and there were times that they'd called her in from the kitchen to get her perspective, as well.

"My wife is a discerning woman," Mark used to say. "And she's discreet. I'd like to hear what she thinks."

After her husband's death, the bishop still came to her from time to time, asking her opinion on issues that might relate to the women of their community, or the young people. Adel had married Mark when she was eighteen, and she hadn't been a frivolous young woman at all. She'd prayed that *Gott* would use her, and His answer had been in her deacon husband. *Gott* hadn't blessed them with *kinner* of their own, but Adel still felt needed and valued. The fact that Bishop Glick came to her for sensitive community issues like this one meant more to her than most people realized.

Adel gathered up the tea things to bring them back into the kitchen.

"Let me show you to your room, Jacob."

"My friends call me Jake," he said.

His friends...the *Englisher* ones? They'd never called him anything but Jacob here in Redemption. She stole another look at Jacob. He was tall, muscular, fit. His face was shaven, as was proper for a single Amish man, but she could make out the gray in the faint stubble on his chin. His face was tanned, and there were lines around his dark eyes that still held a certain playfulness that he'd retained since his youth. He was handsome—there, she'd just admitted it. But she wasn't crossing any lines with him. She wouldn't be calling him Jake.

"Your friends can call you anything they like, but your matchmaker calls you Jacob," Adel replied.

Jacob laughed, the sound low and warm, and she felt goose bumps rise up on her arms at the sound of it. She cast him a faint smile and led the way into the kitchen with the platter. He followed her, his bag in one hand and his hat in the other, and when she placed the platter on the counter, she turned back toward him.

"This is the kitchen, obviously. I always keep some pie, muffins and a few other snacking foods on the counter. No need to ask, just eat what you like. My sister and I have meals ready for a seven o'clock breakfast, twelve noon lunch and a six o'clock dinner."

"Thanks." Jacob glanced around. "This will be very comfortable. I appreciate it."

"Okay, well, let me take you through to your room, then."

The *dawdie* house was actually an extension that had been built onto this home a few decades ago for Mark's elderly parents, who lived there until their passing. It allowed the older people to maintain a little bit of privacy while letting the younger generation take over the main house. The Amish loved to keep family together, but they were also pragmatic about giving couples their own space. Turning the no-longer-used *dawdie* house into a room to rent had been Adel's idea.

The *dawdie* house was connected to the main house on the other end of the kitchen, which was a convenient layout giving her and Naomi privacy upstairs, but also giving their guests full access to food when they were hungry. The kitchen was the center of any home.

She led him into the guest quarters, which

included a small bedroom with wide windows that let in plenty of light, and a sitting room with its own stove for heat, not needed this time of year. Instead, she had the windows wide open to let in some fresh air. Naomi had left a few brochures on the bedside table for local activities that would be of interest to tourists, and Jacob picked them up, leafed through them, then quirked an eyebrow at her.

"I'm not exactly a tourist," he said.

"We put them out for all our guests," she replied. "That must have been Naomi. She wasn't thinking."

Adel ran the bed-and-breakfast with her unmarried sister, and they'd grown much closer over the last few years.

"I am sorry about your uncle," she added. "He would have been like a father to you after your own *daet* died."

"He would have been if he cared to be," Jacob replied. "He and *Daet* never did get along. Nothing like you and Naomi do, it seems."

"Oh, Naomi and I disagree sometimes, too," Adel said. In fact, she and her sister were very different. Naomi was a plump, smiling woman who thought that Adel was far too serious. If Naomi were left to her own devices, she'd have turned them into New

Order Amish within a year, just by concessions and bright new ideas.

"So why do you refuse to get married again?" Jacob asked.

Adel shot him a wry smile. "I am not on your list of potential wives, you know."

"I would never ask you to lower yourself," he said with a teasing grin in return. "I'm curious, though."

"I've already been married," she replied.

"That's all?" he asked.

"That's all." That was all she was willing to tell him, at least. When a woman married, she took on her husband's station in life. She was his helpmeet, and through her marriage to Mark, she'd found her place in this community, and she was deeply satisfied with it. Besides, well-respected widowers weren't in such common supply as many a single woman might wish.

"Why didn't Naomi marry?" he asked.

"She's one of the Good Apples." It was the kind way of saying that she'd been passed over in the marriage market. She was too high on the tree, and while she was wonderful, no one had been able to reach her. That was how they put it delicately.

"Hmm." Jacob nodded.

"And you?" she asked. "You're not a young man anymore, and you're not married, either."

Jacob shrugged. "I was far from home. I wasn't going to marry a girl without a *kapp* and apron, was I?"

"I don't know," she replied. "You didn't come back… You might have wanted to settle down in your *Englisher* life."

Jacob grew more serious. "I might have, too, if I'd met the right woman. But I never did. It's hard to find someone who truly understands you when you're Amish born and they're…not."

"*Yah*, I could see that," she agreed.

But he had stayed far from home for a very long time, and that was worrisome. At any point, he could have come back. *Would* a marriage be enough to keep him here?

Outside, Adel heard the clop of horses' hooves, and she leaned to look out the window. Naomi was back with the groceries, and her curly red hair was coming loose from her *kapp* like it always seemed to do.

"That's my sister," Adel said. "I'll let you settle in. Come into the kitchen when you're ready for something to eat."

"Thank you."

Adel headed out of his room and closed

the door behind her. She let out a little shaky breath, and then headed across the kitchen to the side door to go out and help her sister unhitch the horses. There were no specific men's jobs here—there were no men around to do them.

"How was shopping?" Adel asked as she met Naomi at the horse's side.

"The price of flour went up again," Naomi said. "And the price of sugar."

"It never seems to stop," Adel said. She remembered when Mark used to take care of the money, and Adel hadn't ever worried about the rising prices. What a burden he'd carried all that time, and she'd never known.

"Is he here?" Naomi asked, looking toward the house. She didn't need to specify whom she meant.

"*Yah*, the bishop just left," Adel replied. "Jacob is settling in." She cast her sister a look. "Why did you leave brochures in his room? He's not here as a tourist."

"I don't know," Naomi said with a twinkle in her eye. "He almost feels like one, he's been gone so long."

Adel chuckled. "Well, he's here now, and I've agreed to help find him a wife."

They worked quickly together unhitching

the horses, unbuckling straps and easing the horses out of their tack to send them loose into the field to graze. The sun shone off their glossy backs, and the animals tossed their heads in enjoyment of their freedom.

Naomi opened the gate, and Adel patted their sides to encourage them to head through. They didn't need the encouragement.

Naomi pushed the gate shut again. "I'm just as single as the rest, and a paid-off farm is rather enticing."

"You aren't actually considering marrying Jacob!" Adel said.

"He's a nice-looking man…" Naomi glanced toward the house again and Adel rolled her eyes. "What?"

"Jacob is a risk!" Adel said, lowering her voice. "A big one. He went to the city to work, and just never came back. He wouldn't have come back, either, if it weren't for this inheritance. He'd still be living English. He isn't here because he believes that the Amish life is the best one, because actions speak louder than words. He's back for the land—a personal connection to it or not, that's why he's here."

"Did he say that in so many words?" Naomi asked.

"Not in so many, but…" Adel sighed. "I

admit, I do think he's got good intentions. Don't get me wrong. If he marries an Amish woman, he knows what that means, but will an Amish life ultimately make him happy? What happens if he gets bored of farm life and decides to go back to the city? Would you go with him? Or would you stay on your own and run a farm without him? He might be back, but I'm not so sure that he'll even stay. Good intentions only go so far."

Naomi nodded. "I know, I know. How long do you have to find him a wife?"

"Two weeks."

"Two weeks?" Naomi shook her head.

They headed around to the back of the buggy to get their groceries, and stopped in the shade that it cast.

"You don't sound like you think he's worth marrying," Naomi said.

Adel was silent for a moment. "The bishop thinks he's back for good."

"But what do *you* think?" Naomi pressed. "Because if you're going to sit down with one of our friends and neighbors and tell her that she should take lifelong vows to Jacob Knussli, then you'd better believe he's worth the rest of her life, because I know you. You're honest to a fault, Adel. *To a fault.*"

"I don't take the trust of our community lightly," Adel said. "People look to me to give them the honest truth, and I don't play with that."

Her position in the community wasn't one of a widow looking for a husband. Mark had left her enough money to continue supporting herself, so she didn't have that kind of desperation. And while her husband had passed, people still looked to her for the same insight and advice that she'd provided while he was alive. Their trust was sacred.

"Which is all fine and good," Naomi replied, "but you're not going to succeed in finding him a wife unless you can find something redeemable in him yourself."

Adel let out a slow breath. Her sister was right. She couldn't warn Naomi off him and then foist him on some other unsuspecting woman in their community. The bishop thought that Jacob would stay, but men didn't always have the same insight that women did. Sometimes they were downright blind to the true state of things.

"What do I do?" Adel asked.

Naomi picked up a bag of white sugar and eased it into Adel's arms. "You'll have to spend some time with him."

That was the logical conclusion, of course. Adel waited while Naomi picked up the bag of flour, and together they headed toward the side door. Adel had her work cut out for her.

Chapter Two

Jake didn't have many items of clothing. He took his two shirts out of the bag and opened a closet, where he spotted a few wooden hangers. After shaking out his shirts, he hung them up along with his second pair of pants. When he'd returned to Redemption, the first thing he had to do was get some new clothes, and the bishop's wife had set to sewing immediately along with a couple of the older women in the community and he was set the very next day.

He was grateful—that kind of selfless giving wasn't common out there with the *Englishers*. They saw things differently—they believed in the virtue of self-sufficiency. It made sense, except at the end of the day when a man had provided everything for himself without the help of anyone else, he could pat himself on the back and make some comment about bootstraps, but he had no one to feel grateful toward. It closed doors between people. It didn't open them.

He looked around the little guest room. There was a clock hanging on one white wall and a calendar hanging on the other. The bed had crisp white sheets that smelled ever so faintly of bleach, a thin, faded quilt on top and a foiled chocolate resting on the center of a plump pillow. He smiled, unwrapped it and popped it into his mouth.

A somewhat springy cushioned chair was angled toward the window, outside of which he could see the stable and the chicken coop. Adel had opened the corral door and the horse plodded cooperatively inside. His own horse—or his uncle's, to be completely factual—was already in the corral. His uncle's buggy that he'd been using since his arrival sat empty, its shafts resting on two blocks of wood. A couple of minutes later, he heard the door open and shut, and from the kitchen, he could hear the murmur of women's voices, although he couldn't make out the words. Cupboards clicking closed resonated clearly through the walls.

This was a much nicer room than the one he'd been sleeping in at his uncle's farmhouse. It still felt strange. He'd thought about returning home to Redemption time and time again, and he'd never felt quite ready to let go of everything he'd learned to enjoy in the *Englisher* world. Even now after nearly six months of living Amish again, his fingers itched for a cell phone. He had this undeniable urge to scroll through social media feeds and let his mind go blank, or just turn on a TV and listen to the jangle of a rerun in the background. He was praying for *Gott* to take that away. But here with the Amish, he had nothing but quiet, community and no distraction from facing the reality of his own choices.

All the same, he was hungry.

Jake opened the door and stepped out into a short hallway that led into the kitchen. Adel and Naomi had their backs to him as they put some bags of dried goods up into a cupboard. Adel was slimmer than Naomi, but he'd recognize Naomi's wild curls anywhere.

"Hi, Naomi," Jake said.

Both women turned, and Adel's cheeks were pink. Naomi shot him a grin.

"Hi, Jacob." Naomi put her hands on her hips. "I hear there's a wedding coming up."

If only it were that easy. It seemed less complicated when he'd gotten the call from the lawyer six months ago than it did now.

"Well, we'll see," he replied. "I'm trusting my future to the hands of Adel."

Jake caught Adel's eye, and she picked up a towel and wiped her hands, avoiding his look. Was it possible that he was able to discomfit the perfectly prim Adel? Some primal part of him enjoyed that thought. She had a rather ageless look about her—her skin smooth and creamy, but her eyes holding more experience than she should for her years. And she was distractingly beautiful.

"*Yah*, my sister the matchmaker," Naomi said, shaking her head. "I suppose she does have a lot of experience in marriage, and in working with the community. Still, if she's going to be a matchmaker now, maybe she can find me a nice single man who likes to eat."

"I'm only his matchmaker at the moment," Adel said with a chuckle. "Although it might be a nice new occupation—helping young people find love."

"Young people." Naomi mouthed the words at Jake and rolled her eyes. Naomi was five years younger than Jake and Adel were, making her thirty-two, he realized. None of them as young as they used to be.

"We aren't that old, Adel," he said jokingly. "*I'm* not that old."

"I've buried a husband already," she replied and this time she met his gaze evenly. His humor evaporated.

"Right." He cleared his throat. "I'm sorry."

Adel had gone through more than the rest of them had, and it would have changed her. It certainly explained those eyes that seemed to be brimming with more life experience than anyone else he knew. And maybe she didn't want any reassurances that she was just the same, because she wasn't.

"Naomi and I were talking before we came in," Adel said. "And she had a good point."

Jake glanced toward Naomi, but this time she wasn't joking around.

"We don't really know you anymore," Naomi said.

"And I should know you a lot better if I'm going to introduce you as a potential husband for a woman in this community," Adel added.

"That's fair," he agreed. "What did you have in mind?"

"Well, we are rather stuck for time," Adel said. "We're hosting an Amish tour that is coming through this evening, but Naomi can take care of that, I think. Why don't we have an early supper, and then you and I can go take a look at your family's farm? The more information I have, the better."

"I don't make sense to you, do I?" he asked.

"No, you don't," she agreed.

He nodded, and a smile toyed at his lips. "The feeling is mutual."

Adel was beautiful, soft, intelligent and running her own bed-and-breakfast. She was trusted with sensitive situations by the bishop. But she was choosing a single life, not a choice that many Amish women made voluntarily. She was a tangle of contradictions.

"Well…" Adel turned toward the cupboards. "Let's get something to eat, and then we can head out."

The horse, a ten-year-old Clydesdale named Samson, pulled the buggy easily without even seeming to notice the extra weight behind him. He plodded along, his tail swishing in the evening breeze, and Jake leaned back, the reins loose in his hands.

Adel was here to size him up. It was her job to judge him, figure him out, decide if he was worthy enough for one of their local women. This shouldn't annoy him, but it did just a little bit.

"Is there anyone you're interested in?" Adel asked. "You've been back for a few months. Are there any single women who have caught your eye?"

"I've talked to some," he said. He rattled off a few names. "But if there wasn't a spark without a farm, it's a little insulting to try again with one, you know?"

She nodded. "That's understandable. Does this scare you at all, having to choose a woman this quickly—vow to love and take care of her for the rest of your life after knowing her a matter of days?"

He cast her a wry smile. "Yes. Very much."

"Then why are you doing it?" she asked.

Jake let out a slow breath. "I grew up on that farm. I was born there. I've worked the last few months to put it back together again, and it's been a huge amount of work."

He thought back to his childhood after his mother passed away. It had been just the three of them—*Daet*, Uncle Johannes and Jake. They'd worked the farm together, and kept house together, too. Their house had started to get cluttered right away without a woman living with them. Women didn't like clutter—they picked things up, put them away, set them aside to be brought to someone else who could use them. But without *Mamm*, Jake, his father and his uncle used to sit by the woodstove during cold evenings, and Uncle Johannes would read aloud from the *Budget* newspaper, updating them on all the goings-on in the surrounding communities. Something had obviously gone very wrong, however, because a cluttered farmhouse had turned into a farmhouse that was alarmingly full of things—old copies of the *Budget*, stacks of milk bottle crates, worn-out shoes that were piled up in pairs, empty bailing twine spools…from floorboards to rafters, the house was simply full.

"I couldn't wait to get out of Redemption when I was a teenager," he went on. "The tension between my *daet* and uncle was unbearable. I took that factory job in the city knowing full well it wasn't the kind of place a good Amish man lived, but it got me off that farm and gave me a chance to build something of my own." Jake batted a swarm of tiny flies away from his face. "But it's funny— you can't start over as easily as you think. That land is Knussli land. It belonged to my great-grandfather, my grandfather, my uncle… I never knew how to come home, but my uncle's frustrating will gave me a reason to try. If I don't get that land back, I'm losing a bigger part of myself than I ever realized. I'm Amish. I might be disillusioned, and I might have some tough memories, but it's who I am. That land is part of my heritage."

"Didn't you at least try to talk to your *daet* or your uncle?" Adel asked.

His mind went back to those difficult years. "I used to meet up with Alphie for a coffee in town, and he'd fill me in on the family drama."

"What kind of drama?" she asked.

"Oh, just how they felt about me after I left, things they were saying when they saw Alphie—that kind of thing."

"So you didn't talk to your *daet*?" she asked.

"My *daet* was telling everyone else that he was so deeply disappointed in me that he didn't want to see me unless I was fully penitent," he replied.

"I honestly never heard him say anything like that," Adel said. "All I ever heard your *daet* say was how he missed you."

Jake's gaze flickered in her direction. "Really?"

"Yah." She eyed him. "Are you telling me

that you stayed away because of what Alphie was telling you?"

Jake swung his attention out the other side of the buggy, shielding his face from view. "He was sympathetic to my situation. He understood better than anyone else did."

"I'm sorry to say this, Jake, but if he was so sympathetic to what you were going through, he should have helped you to fix your relationship with your *daet* while you still had time."

"That did occur to me a few times," Jake said. "After the funeral, I tried to talk to my uncle, but it was no use. Alphie had been right about his attitude, so I figured he had probably been right about my *daet*'s, too."

"And now?" she asked. "Johannes left you the farm. I mean, he didn't make it easy, but he could just as easily have left it to Alphie."

"Yah..." He sighed. "I shouldn't have been listening to my cousin instead of talking to people directly. I was being a coward. I didn't want to face their anger. And that was both wrong of me and cowardly."

"Was Alphie talking to Johannes and your father on your behalf, too?" she asked.

"Not that I asked him to, but I suppose that's how it works when someone is in the middle, isn't it?" He shot her a forlorn look. "I made a mistake. I should have come back sooner and faced my own father. I should have."

"Are you close with Alphie now?" she asked.

"We talked a bit over the last few month, but—" He sighed. "I'm not foolish enough to empty my heart to him again. Besides, we're now in competition for that land, aren't we? If I can't get married, he gets it." He was silent for a moment. "But you know, I don't think Alphie was trying to do any damage. I think my leaving was the most interesting thing going on here in Redemption, and he got the inside scoop on it. He didn't mean harm..."

"But he also wasn't trying to fix it," she countered. "He wasn't making peace."

"True." He pressed his lips together grimly. "I'll have to sort things out with my cousin one of these days. Eventually. I haven't gotten there yet."

"I think you should," she said.

"The thing is, I stayed away because I didn't want to face all the judgment and anger that I was sure was waiting for me, and the longer you stay away, the more you slide into a completely different way of life. I mean, I started out using electricity for the stove and fridge—because it was a rental, and anything else wouldn't be allowed. And after a year, I had a cell phone, a TV, a laptop computer… And every single one of them had come with a very sincere excuse, you know?"

"I suppose that's how it works," she said.

"I never meant to slide that far. But when you're out there, it makes sense. It's just…life."

"It didn't feel empty? Wrong?" she asked.

"No. It was just how people lived. It was how they worked in their community. People communicated with phones and internet. They got to each other's homes in cars and buses. It didn't feel wrong."

"Does it feel wrong now?" she asked softly.

He wouldn't lie. "No. I mean, it isn't part of the Amish life that I'm choosing, but *wrong* is a strong word. Let's say it isn't something I'm choosing."

He was talking too much. He hadn't actually intended to say so much, but besides the bishop, Adel was the first person he'd encountered in years who'd asked, or who understood how different his life had become.

"That was all rather personal," he added, and he glanced over at her to find her softened gaze locked on him. "I'm not trying to put you into the middle here, either. I—"

"I'm used to keeping confidences," she said quietly.

That's right—she had been the deacon's wife, and there was something of that role that had stuck to her.

"I have to admit," he said. "My family problems aside, what I want most is to find a woman I fall in love with—hat over boot nails. That's why I waited so long to tell anyone about that part of the will. I wanted a woman to fall for me without the money as incentive. But I'm running out of time, so maybe it'll happen, like Isaac and Rebecca did in the Bible—with an introduction."

"You think *Gott* is working in mysterious ways?" she asked.

"Well, I'm back in Redemption, aren't I?" Jake shrugged. "And after everything that's happened, if that isn't *Gott* working, I don't know what is."

They came up over a hill, and tumbling across the landscape was the familiar patchwork of the Knussli family farm. There was a field of oats flanked by another field of wheat, and the pasture for what used to be a rather large herd, but now was only about thirty head of cattle. The red barn was worn, and even from this distance he could see the gray smudges against the red paint. The sun was lowering, the rays were long and golden, warming up the entire scene below them, and Jake's heart gave a squeeze.

Home. For better or for worse, this farm was the place that held his childhood memories, his adolescent hopes, and those dreams he used to have when lying in the bedroom of that apartment in the city, the ones where he could smell the country air and it was more real than even being there. He'd hated this place at some points in his life, and he'd loved it in equal measure, but it was home.

Adel waited as Jacob unhitched the horse and she surveyed the front yard. It needed work—a flower garden seemed to have been abandoned years ago, because she could see some ornamental onion and catmint flowers scattered around the grass that hadn't been mown in some time. Once upon a time, those perennial flowers would have been corralled in a little garden instead of traveling across the yard. There had been a woman here—Jacob's mother. But that was long ago, and if all went according to the bishop's plans, at least, there would be a woman here again soon. It only seemed right. This place was badly in need of a wife's touch.

The house was covered in a yellow tent—

the work of the fumigators—but beyond, she could see the stable, the barn, a chicken house and even a covered area for storing hay farther on. It was a decent farm.

Adel looked back toward Jacob. His Amish clothes fit him well with his broad shoulders, and he had an easy way of standing with all his weight on one leg that made her recognize just how handsome he was. That was something she'd noticed repeatedly over the last few months since his return. Jacob was handsome in a way that tugged at her. This last decade seemed to have hardened Jake, though, solidified him into a more powerful version of himself. He wasn't a safe Amish man, but he was attractive. She shouldn't be noticing that—not the way she was, at least. If he was an attractive option for another woman, that was good. But not for her.

Jacob had finished with the horse, and he had both thumbs in his suspenders, looking out across the fields. As if he could feel her scrutiny, he suddenly turned toward her, his dark gaze catching hers. She felt her cheeks heat, and she smoothed her apron down—a nervous gesture. He jutted his chin toward the fields in a silent invitation, and a smile quirked up one side of his mouth.

Adel headed in his direction, and she fell into step beside him as he led the way. They went out a side gate that he secured behind them after Adel had passed through. She could see him relaxing as he walked.

"The barn needs a lot of work," Jacob said. "More than just a paint job. The roof needs to be redone."

"Hmm." Adel nodded. "But you could take care of that easily enough."

"*Yah*, I can replace a roof. I decided to wait until it's mine, though. I've invested enough of my own money into making this place more livable, but I don't want to put in too much if it's not going to be mine, you know? Alphie can deal with new roofs if he's going to inherit it." He slowed to a stop, his gaze locked on the barn. "Do you want to see inside?"

"I suppose," she replied.

Adel followed his lead, and they headed in that direction.

"A wife will be spending most of her time in the house, though," she said.

"*Yah*, but I can't show you inside there right now. Besides, I think a woman could appreciate a farm that can support itself, too," Jacob replied. "Can't she?"

"Of course."

"The house needs a lot of work, though. I've cleaned up some of it. My uncle never did fix it up inside, and he filled it up with all sorts of trash. I don't know what happened, because when it was the three of us, we kept things in pretty good repair. I mean, it was cluttered, but it wasn't as bad as I found it."

"Your cousin didn't warn you about that?" she asked.

"Not a word." He pressed his lips together in a look of frustration. "I don't suppose a woman looks forward to coming to a run-down house, an unstocked kitchen and rooms that are still filled with garbage."

"You didn't manage to clean it out?" she asked.

"I was running the farm on my own." He sighed. "I managed to clean out some of it. Not enough."

He dropped his gaze, and she could see the shame shining in his eyes. But it wasn't his fault. He'd come home to this mess—he hadn't created it himself.

"A good woman will take it as a challenge and make a home out of it," Adel said with more certainty than she felt.

"But if a woman is accepting a rushed marriage proposal, the very least she could expect is a decent kitchen," Jacob said.

They arrived at the barn, and he pulled the door wide and stepped inside first, holding it open for her behind him. He strode inside, turned in a full circle, then pulled off his hat and looked upward. His not-quite-Amish haircut was still disconcerting for her.

"The struts are still good," Jacob said. "See?"

She looked up, mostly out of a cooperative instinct, but apparently she wasn't looking in the right place because he sighed audibly and came up beside her. He put warm hands on her shoulders, pivoting her, and directed her attention upward.

"There—" He pointed at the beams that braced the roof. "Still strong."

He didn't move his hands right away, and she found herself enjoying the warm gentleness of his touch. Then his hands fell away from her shoulders, and she let out a cautious breath.

"When I was about ten, I climbed up there from the hayloft," Jake said. "I used to like to read up there, so high above everything. I fell one evening and broke my collarbone. That was after my mom died."

"Ouch," she murmured, then paused before asking, "How old were you when your mother died?"

"Eight." He glanced toward her, then shrugged. "And you're probably thinking that if I had a mother at home, she wouldn't have let me do that. And you'd be right."

"What was she like?" Adel asked.

"I don't remember much." He glanced over at her, his expression thoughtful. "The *Englishers* have photos. I know we don't do that, but what I wouldn't give for a picture of my *mamm* right about now…"

"You must remember something, though," she said.

"I do. I remember the kitchen being brighter, and everything being cleaner. I remember sunlight feeling warmer, and birdsong being sweeter… There was just something about those years when we had *mamm* that made everything better." He licked his lips, then shrugged. "I have a couple of concrete memories. One of them, I must have been pretty young, because I remember playing with her apron strings and her mixing something in this white bowl with a red stripe around it. She used that bowl for everything. I remember her hands, too. Her fingers were always cool, and that felt nice on my head when I was sick… I remember lying in my bed upstairs, and listening to my mother sing while she worked."

"That's beautiful."

"She was a terrible singer." Jacob chuckled. "It's a nice memory now, but she was so off-key, and she never seemed to know."

"Maybe she didn't care," Adel replied.

Jacob shrugged in acceptance. "When *Mamm* died, things changed right away. I had some aunts who would come by and keep the garden, do some cooking, do our laundry... But that couldn't last forever. We figured out how to keep things running, but we did it in a man's way."

"What's a man's way?" she asked.

"The cooking is quicker, I'll tell you that," he said. "Lots of stews and pots of soup. As for laundry, I don't think we ever got our whites all the way white again. And my *daet* and uncle didn't much care if I climbed up to the rafters in the barn, so long as I got my chores done."

"It sounds very lonely."

"You don't see too many Amish only-child families, do you?" The joking was back in his eyes. He was backing away from the personal memories. "I had no siblings to tell on me."

A younger sibling was an early warning

system for all sorts of shenanigans. Being the fourth of eight children in her family, she'd been both the tattler and the annoyed older sibling in that arrangement. But Jacob's childhood had been exceptionally solitary.

"Come on," he said. "I'm just getting a feel for the state of the place. If it's going to be mine, I'll need to get to work on getting it back into shape."

She saw the way his eyes lit up as he said it, and she had to wonder what would happen if this farm didn't come to him. How much would that hurt?

"Will you stay in Redemption if you don't get the farm?" she asked.

Jacob rubbed a hand over his chin, his gaze still moving over the inside of the barn. "That's something to think about, isn't it? I'd have to face Alphie having the land that should have been mine..."

But he didn't finish the thought.

"The answer to that matters," she said quietly. She needed a clear understanding of where he stood.

Jacob glanced down at her. "I don't like this balance between us, Adel."

"What balance?" she asked. "I'm your matchmaker."

"You were my schoolmate," he replied.

"We're a long way from school days, Jacob."

"I'm Jake!" He shook his head. "Adel, I'm Jake… Say it."

"Jake," she conceded.

"Thank you." He scrubbed a hand through his hair and replaced his hat. "And while you're perfectly comfortable there trying to figure me out, I don't like this. You're just as much of a puzzle to me, you know."

"Me?" Adel put her hands on her hips. "There's nothing to sort out. I'm widowed, and I've been asked to help you find a wife. That's all that matters."

"Widowed—" He waggled a finger at her. "You use that as a very convenient shield. You can cut off any conversation that gets uncomfortable for you by pulling that up. You lost your husband—discussion over."

"What discussion, Jacob?" She winced. "I mean, Jake…"

"Maybe I want a few answers from you, as well," he said.

"Like what?"

"Like why *you're* still single," he said.

Her heart skipped a beat, and she forced what she hoped was an easy smile. "I told you. I've already been married."

This was her well-thought-out answer. It had sufficed for everyone else…

"But that doesn't add up. You're still young. Your life is over?" He shook his head. "One wedding, you tragically lose your husband, and you shut down for the rest of your life?"

"I haven't shut down!" Her anger was rising now, too. "I have a life here! I'm respected! I'm a part of things!"

"And you wouldn't be if you got married again?" He crossed his arms, watching her face a little too closely for her liking. "We're Amish. Life centers on family—marriages, kids…"

"I gained something with my marriage to Mark," she said, and she pressed her lips together. She didn't want to talk to him about that.

"Respect," he said.

So he'd noticed? She let out a slow breath. "Yes."

"And you think you'd lose that if you married someone else."

"I wouldn't be the deacon's wife anymore, would I?" she said. "Or the deacon's widow. I'd be someone else's wife."

"Is that such a bad thing?" he asked. He waited a beat, then he nodded. "I see."

"You see what?" she asked.

"Adel." He leaned closer. "You're a snob."

"What?" She felt the blood rush from her face. "I am no such thing!"

"Yes, you are," he said. "You don't want to be some humble farmer's wife, or the wife of a shopkeeper. You don't want to be a stepmother, either, I imagine. You like being the woman that the community looks to for wisdom and insight into things. You'd rather be the woman who lives alone with the community's awe than one who pours all that energy into her own home. You like the *position*."

"That is not the Amish way," she said tartly. "You may have forgotten."

"We may be Amish and live by our ideals, but we're human, too, Adel."

"You've been away a long time," she countered. "Maybe that's the *Englisher* way of seeing things seeping in."

"*You're* human, Adel." His voice dropped, and he didn't look cowed, or derailed. He took a step closer to her, and she felt her breath catch in her throat. He didn't scare her, but she was rather struck by the size of him.

"I'm not arguing about whether or not I'm human," she said. "I'm flesh and blood like you are, but that doesn't mean I'm a snob, either! I have the right to choose who I marry, if I marry, and whether or not I want to dedicate my life to any particular man!" Her voice shook. "It is not my duty to keep house and raise the children of any man who needs a wife. It is my duty, however, to live the life *Gott* gave me with as much faith, hope and charity that I can!"

Jake nodded. "Agreed."

"Really?" She was prepared for more argument than that, and she halfway wished he'd put up more of a fight, because she was ready to give him one.

"You don't have to take on any man as your duty in life," he said. "I fully agree with that. But you also don't have to hide behind your widowhood, either."

"It isn't hiding," she said simply. "You're right—my marriage to Mark did change things. But it isn't snobbery. When Mark and I weren't able to have *kinner*, I prayed that *Gott* would use me in a different way. And He did! Without babies of my own to care for, I was available to help others in their times of need. I could be there for women when they were struggling with their own difficulties. I was able to be there for children who needed to talk things out, or teenagers who were frustrated with our rules. Do you know how they say that if we could see the path *Gott* planned for us, we'd never choose a different one?"

"*Yah.*" Jake's dark gaze was still locked on her face.

"I wouldn't choose a different one, Jake," she said quietly. "It's more fulfilling than I ever dreamed to be a part of things this way. I don't want to take on another husband or his children. You're right. I don't want it. I want to see what *Gott* has on this path He set me on."

"Maybe you'll end up being Redemption's official matchmaker," he said.

"Maybe. But I'm not a snob."

It mattered to Adel that he know that. She didn't think she was better than anyone, but sometimes *Gott* put people on the outside of the circle for a reason.

"You're not a snob," he said quietly. "I'm sorry I said it."

"Thank you."

"But this isn't going to be a one-way street, either," he said with a smile touching his lips. "You'll be digging into my life, but I'm going to figure you out, too, Adel."

Adel rolled her eyes. "You can try, but we don't have much time to find you a legal wife. We're better off keeping to our mission."

The grin he shot her suggested that he'd just accepted a challenge, and somehow she doubted it was only about finding his wife.

Were all bachelors this difficult? If her goal was to become the matchmaker around here, she might be taking on more trouble than she ever imagined.

Chapter Three

Jake took one more look up at the barn roof. He could see the sections that were weak and would leak like a colander again during the next big rainstorm. He'd already stretched big, blue tarps over the hay and supplies that lay beneath them, and he felt a wave of frustration toward his late uncle.

Or had Johannes's health been failing for longer than anyone knew? He couldn't help the nagging sense of guilt that if Jake had at least visited, he would have known if his uncle needed more help than he'd been able to hire. Uncle Johannes hadn't been an easy man to deal with, but he'd been family. Jake could have come to his aid.

But he couldn't change that now. Jake nodded toward the barn door.

"So, more about you—" Jake said, holding the barn door open for her as they went back outside into the summer sunlight.

"You're serious about trying to figure me out?" she asked.

The sun felt good on his shoulders, and he led the way up to the fence that separated pasture from the barnyard. He gave the rails a shake, and a few were loose. Jake looked down the line of fencing. He'd already fixed some broken sections, and now it was sturdy.

"Who tried to court you after your husband died?" he asked, turning back toward her.

She blinked at him, then swallowed. By her reaction, he'd hit on it, it seemed.

"What do you mean?" she asked.

As if he didn't know anything about how men thought. The single men would have taken notice when Adel became a widow.

"It was someone," Jake said, and when she looked ready to protest, he added, "I'm looking at you, Adel, and you're gorgeous. Forgive me for saying it so bluntly—that's admittedly very English of me to do—but you are not a woman who'd just melt into the background. You never were. So knowing how men work, I know that there would have been men who tried to court you. There's no question about that. I'm just curious who it was."

She smiled faintly. "You flatter me."

"Not at all," he replied soberly. "I tell the truth. And I'm right, aren't I?"

She gave him one of those sidelong looks he was growing to associate with her. "Two men, actually. First, there was Duncan Huyard, who's five years younger than me and couldn't hold down a job to save his life."

"Ouch." Jake cast her a sympathetic look. "Not any woman's ideal. Was there pressure for you to accept him?"

Adel shook her head. "No, everyone knew why I didn't want to marry him. But it was the second one who tried courting me, Abner Graber, that everyone thought I should accept."

Abner… An image rose in his mind of a meaty, tall man with a round, unfriendly face. He was older than they were, and very stern. That was all that Jake remembered of him.

"Didn't he marry that young woman—"

"Susanna, *yah*," Adel said. "They had six *kinner* in five years—two sets of twins. She died in childbirth with the last baby—it was born prematurely six months after her last birth."

Jake's heart stopped in his chest. "What?"

That math was…cruel. What husband didn't think about those things?

"*Yah*… Abner wanted a houseful of *kinner*, and I don't think he cared one bit about the health of that poor girl he married. Anyway, regardless of those circumstances, he was in want of a wife, and he thought I would do nicely to take care of those six *kinner* for him."

He could see the flutter of her pulse at the base of her neck and the way her cheeks paled—that marriage proposal had scared her, and he could understand why.

"He wouldn't have been a good husband," Jake confirmed.

"Not everyone agreed with that, though. He works hard," she said. "He has a well-kept farm. His wife never lacked for material for sewing or food in her pantry."

But he was a bully.

"No one else saw the warning signs in Abner?" he asked.

"Maybe they didn't think I had any reason to complain," she replied. "I was widowed and in need of a husband. He was a widower in need of a wife. He was a hard worker, and so was I. They saw no problem."

"Maybe they thought you'd improve him," he said.

"If they thought that, they were being very foolish, indeed." Adel paused. "Did no one try to get *you* married?"

"Oh, my *daet* asked me to come home and meet a nice girl a couple of times," he replied. He remembered the letters—the pleading between the lines. But he couldn't do it. Taking a wife was a huge responsibility both financially and emotionally. He couldn't just choose a nice girl and decide to love her.

But that was what he was doing now, wasn't it?

"You never did come back and look for a girl, though," Adel said. "Not that I saw."

"I wasn't ready," he replied.

"Are you now?" she asked.

Jake sobered. That was a good question. Because the responsibility hadn't changed. He'd need to provide for a wife, and for their *kinner*. He'd need to be there for her emotionally, too, and make her happy on a heart level. That was harder to guarantee.

But all the same, when he thought about this farm, it wasn't from the days of just the three men running things. It was a whisper from the past that tugged at him, a time when the house was filled with baking and a woman's laughter. It was from a time when brilliantly white laundry fluttered out on the line.

"I'm ready to have a bright kitchen again," he said quietly. "I'm ready to have a woman's touch in my home, and her cooking on the table. I'm ready to hear singing when she doesn't know I'm listening..."

He cleared his throat. That was too much— why did he keep doing that? When he looked over at Adel, he saw sympathy in her eyes.

"A woman is the heart of a home," he said. "I'm no fool."

And whether he was ready to be the husband and father a family needed no longer mattered. There was a beautiful life waiting for a man who was willing to step up and take it, but it did require a step up. A man couldn't drag a woman down to his level. He had to accept the responsibilities that came with a family and become the stable provider they needed.

With this farm, he could do it.

Without the farm? He felt a dark cloud at the prospect of losing this land, and he knew that was dangerous. But if he didn't have the family farm, he'd be back at the beginning again, with the best-paying job he could get being in the city. So *yah*, he was ready for a wife and family, but he was afraid to want it too badly. The longing began in a place that was too deep. That disappointment would hurt if it didn't work out.

Jake looked down to see Adel leaning against the fence next to him. The sun shone off the bit of hair that was visible, and she smelled sweet, but what made women smell that way, he didn't know. It was like they were from a different world, almost.

"I'm going to tell you the truth," he said quietly. "The house is in bad shape. There's a whole bedroom filled up with junk, and most of the dishes are broken and thrown out, so I think there's about four plates all together that are left, and some big pots that have been burned too often. My uncle repaired some cushions on the couch with duct tape..." He looked down at Adel thoughtfully. "I was glad that the fumigation wasn't done yet, because I didn't want to show you that."

There were a lot of painful, tender places in his memory that he didn't want to show her, too. He wasn't the most polished-up man, either. He'd run away from the family *Gott* gave him, and backslid down to living like a common *Englisher*. Whoever married him was going to get the sad reality, in both house and husband.

"It's probably best to be up-front about the state of the house," Adel said.

"I suppose so," he agreed. "But it won't endear her to me, I'm sure."

"You said you wanted love," she said. "If a woman loves you, she'll roll up her sleeves."

Jake looked down at her. *"Yah?"*

"Yah." She nodded. "But love… That's not something I can guarantee, is it? I can work to find you a wife, but it'll be up to you to secure her heart."

Jake looked back out at the cows, his thoughts in tangles. He could see the reason why this community saw Adel as a wise woman. She had more answers than he did.

"All the same, I'd like to clean out the kitchen, at least," he said. "I haven't done that yet. I'm more comfortable fixing fences and tending cattle."

"Fixing the kitchen would be nice," she said.

"Even if I'm cleaning it out for Alphie," he said ruefully. "There will be a woman in that kitchen eventually, and leaving it in the state it's in feels wrong."

"You're a decent man," she said.

"Decent enough to put your conscience at

ease about recommending me as a husband to some local woman?" he asked.

"Yah." Her eyes crinkled as she smiled, and she shaded her eyes to look up at him. "I think you'll do nicely. It's a matter of picking the right woman now."

Adel seemed a little gentler, less reserved. Was that because she'd decided he wasn't quite the danger she had suspected? Or was she just feeling sorry for him?

"Thank you," he said.

And here was hoping that *Gott* was using this for His own purposes, because a marriage was for life, and this decision would be a fast one. It would be awful to marry a woman and find himself in an unhappy union for the rest of his life for the sake of this land.

This farm might be his home, but a woman would be its beating heart.

Back at the house, Adel checked the chicken legs in the oven. Naomi made a delicious homemade barbecue sauce, and the meat was roasting gently, the aroma making Adel's stomach grumble. The tour group had already come and left, and Naomi stood at the kitchen sink washing plates from their visit.

Jake's words had stuck with her, though,

about the things he was ready for in his life. He wanted the beauty back—the feminine touch about a home—and that had stabbed at her heart. How much had Jake suffered when the community didn't see? There were times when privacy covered up pain, like in the case of Abner's young wife. Adel needed to learn from this, and be more vigilant.

"I sold about fifteen jars of jam," Naomi said, pulling Adel's attention back. "So that, added to the fee from the tour group, made it a successful day."

"Did you write it all out in our ledger?" Adel asked.

Naomi cast her a long-suffering look. "*Yah*, Adel."

Adel chuckled. "Sorry. Of course you did."

"What has you stressed?" Naomi asked. "You only start trying to control every detail when you're upset about something."

"I'm not upset, but I am realizing just how big of a job this is to find a wife for Jake," Adel said. "He's been through a lot, and he'll need a wife who will understand him on a heart level."

"He needs a legal wife who will get him that farm," Naomi countered. "That's what this is about."

"It's more than that," Adel replied. "He wants…a real marriage."

"In two weeks?" Naomi shook her head. "That's asking a lot."

"All the same, those vows are for life. It's best to enter into a marriage soberly," she replied.

The women exchanged a silent look, and Naomi turned back to washing the dishes.

"If I recall, you didn't know Mark very well when you married him," Naomi said. She rinsed a dish and put it in the rack.

Adel thought back to when she'd met Mark. It had all been very proper. He was fifteen years older than she was, and he'd been introduced to her at a wedding. They'd talked for a few minutes, and he'd asked if he could see her again. He'd called on her a few times, visits with her parents in the room, and then he'd asked her out for a buggy ride where he'd proposed. Somehow, none of it had seemed frightening. He'd always been respectful of her feelings and listening attentively when she talked. He'd had a dry sense of humor, and he'd never treated her as if she wouldn't understand his jokes. Adel had liked Mark from the start—he was funny, thoughtful and gentle. There was nothing to be scared of in a husband like that.

Would other women feel the same way about Jake, though? He was physically much bigger than Mark had been, and his personality was stronger. He had a way of looking at Adel that locked her to the spot. There was nothing gentle and unassuming about Jake. He was all testosterone and longing.

"Mark was different," Adel said. "He was very gentle by nature, and very thoughtful and bookish. If he wasn't out with the horses, he was reading."

"Well, what is a woman looking for in a husband?" Naomi pulled the plug in the sink and turned around to face Adel as she dried her hands. "She needs a man who will provide, and that farm will do the trick."

"She'll be looking for a good father for her children, too," Adel added.

"*Yah*, that's important. And a man who will be faithfully Amish." They exchanged another look. "Will he stay in the community?"

Adel lifted a lid on a pot on the stove, looking down into a bubbling pot of potatoes. "I think so, but he's got his own views on things. He'll be Amish, but he won't be staunch, if you know what I mean."

"What views?" Naomi asked.

"He's lived with the *Englishers* for a long

time," Adel said. "He doesn't have the aversion to *Englisher* ways that might feel a little safer."

"He is a good-looking man, though," Naomi said. "Very good-looking."

Adel felt her cheeks warm. He was—there was no denying it. "Looks aren't everything, Naomi."

"Perhaps not, but I happen to think that marriage is about more than raising *kinner*," Naomi replied. "It's about the time together as a husband and wife, too."

Adel let out a slow breath. "Before I told you that you shouldn't consider Jake for yourself, and I think I was wrong. If you're interested in him, I could see what he thinks about you."

"Me?" Naomi laughed and shook her head. "No, not me."

"You've changed your mind?" she asked.

"Yes, I have."

"Because he's a risk," Adel agreed.

"No, not because of that." Naomi took some dinner plates out of the cupboard and headed toward their thick, wooden kitchen table. "I'd be stupid indeed to even consider a man who looked at another woman the way he does."

Adel frowned. "He ogles women? I didn't see that."

This might change things. Had she missed out on some glaring character flaws, blinded by her own softening feelings for the man?

"Adel, he doesn't look at other women in the plural," Naomi said, casting her a smile. "He looks at you."

"Me?" Adel shook her head. "I drive him crazy, and he doesn't like that I'm the one set up as judge over him in finding him a wife."

"All of that might be true," Naomi replied. "But he looks at you like... He looks at you the way a man working in the sun all day looks at a tall glass of water."

A smile turned up her sister's lips, and Naomi's eyes sparkled with repressed laughter.

Adel blinked at her sister. "That's not true."

"You think I'd pass up on a hand-delivered husband complete with a paid-off farm for nothing?" Naomi shook her head. "You might not be interested in him, Adel, but I'm not tying myself for life to a man who looks at my sister like *that*."

"I'm sorry, if I—" Adel started.

"Adel, I'm not upset," Naomi said. "I honestly think you should consider him for yourself."

That was easy enough for her sister to say. But Adel had no interest in tying herself to a new husband right now, either. She'd gone five years in this new path of hers that fulfilled her in this strange, unexpected way, and simply giving it up because a man came along who was handsome and in need of a wife didn't change anything.

"Not me," Adel replied. "But I will find him a good woman. He deserves that much."

Naomi nodded. "Do you have anyone in mind?"

"Verna Kauffman is about the right age, and she's never been married," Adel said.

Naomi was silent.

"Delia Swarey needs a *daet* for her four boys," Adel went on. "They've been taking care of things on their own, but they'll be grown and getting married soon enough. She needs a husband of her own again."

"And the younger women?" Naomi asked.

Adel firmly shook her head. "The thing with the young women is that they have every opportunity to find a boy they know well, and do things the old-fashioned way. They should have that chance to get to know someone, and be courted... Because marriage isn't easy, and going from a first meeting to man and

wife in a matter of a week will not be easy
on anyone. That isn't fair to a girl with her
whole life ahead of her."

The thought of a girl of eighteen walking
into a run-down mess of a house was heartbreaking to even consider. Adel had gotten
married that young, but Mark had been prepared. There had been a lovely kitchen waiting for her, all clean and organized by her
mother-in-law.

But nothing was going to be properly ready
for this wife, and while a community would
pitch in to help get things spruced back up
if they found out Jake needed it, that would
take time. And it would take a special kind of
strength from the woman who stepped into
marriage that way.

Strength, or foolhardiness, Adel wasn't
sure which. It would be a risk, that much she
was sure of.

Adel went back to the stove to check the
potatoes, and on her way past the window, she
looked outside to see Jake walking back down
the drive toward the house. He moved with
the easy grace of a man who worked with his
hands, and he fiddled with one side of his suspenders as if they weren't quite comfortable.

Jacob Knussli was certainly a good-looking man, but he would be a hard one to match if Adel wanted to do the job properly. And she did want to find him the right match. He deserved to be understood, appreciated and loved.

Just then, Jake lifted his gaze, and he spotted her. She had the urge to jump out of his line of sight, but she stopped herself. She wasn't some girl watching cute boys. She was his matchmaker, and she'd best act the part, even when she felt least qualified. He didn't smile, but his expression softened, and he reached up and touched the edge of his hat in a hello.

Adel felt Naomi's arm brush against hers as she looked out the window over her shoulder.

"*Yah*, that's the look," Naomi said with a low laugh, and she carried on to the oven, pulling on oven mitts. "I'd be foolish indeed, Adel."

Chapter Four

Adel and Naomi served the meal—mashed potatoes, chicken legs, coleslaw and brown buttered noodles. She had put a little extra effort into this meal, if she was forced to admit it, but it felt worth the work seeing Jake polish off three full platefuls of food.

Adel scooped up the last of the mashed potatoes into the spoon and held them invitingly toward Jake.

"Will you eat the last of them?" she asked.

"No, no, I couldn't eat another bite. But I might come finish them up tonight sometime."

Adel smiled. "Feel free."

"You two really put on a spread," Jake said. "Your bed-and-breakfast must be popular around here."

"We have a steady flow of guests," Naomi said. "We had some guests cancel at the last minute, though, which meant there was space for you."

"So who comes?" he asked.

"Englishers," Adel replied. "Mostly. They stay here and see the sights."

"Couples?" he asked. "Families?"

"Some families," Naomi said, and she took another spoon of coleslaw for herself. "But mostly couples. We're considered quite a romantic spot."

"Are you?" Jake shot Adel a teasing smile. "Should I be surprised? I suppose you are a matchmaker now."

Adel stood up and collected the plates. "I run a business. I'm glad if my guests enjoy themselves."

"What about the couple who got engaged here?" Naomi said. "Last summer, a young man brought his sweetheart here for a dinner, and right here in this room, he got down on one knee and pulled out a ring. Adel got all teary."

"Well, engagements are a beautiful thing," Adel said.

"You're in the right business, Adel," Jake said with a grin. "Love follows wherever you go. I'm in good hands."

Adel carried the plates to the sink. "I do my best."

"I've been telling Adel we should advertise ourselves as a romantic spot," Naomi said. "But she won't do it."

"It isn't proper," Adel replied. She turned in time to see Naomi mouthing her words back at Jake.

"Naomi, you aren't helping," Adel said, annoyed. "I run a proper Amish place. We serve meals, and we have overnight guests, and we give people a glimpse into our way of life. And we Amish don't advertise our romance."

Jake leaned his elbows on the table and met her gaze. "Well, unless we're trying to match a couple up. And then, there's a certain amount of advertising…"

Adel sighed. He wanted to banter, and this wasn't helping! He was handsome, and funny, and interesting to talk to, and that was all well and good for the woman he'd marry to enjoy, but Adel didn't want his direct, warm attention.

"I think it's my turn to take care of the horses," Adel said.

"*Yah*, it is," Naomi replied. "I'll take care of the kitchen."

"Have some pie," Adel said, casting Jake a

smile. "Naomi makes a wonderful peach pie. I think we have some left."

Outside, the evening was cooling off, and a grass-scented breeze came in over the field. Adel let herself into the stable and left the door open to let the breeze come inside. She exhaled a sigh. What was it about Jake Knussli that left her feeling so scattered? She didn't get this way with anyone else. And it wasn't that Jake was being inappropriate, really. He was just being charming.

"Why does that bother me so much?" she muttered aloud.

It threw her off-balance, somehow, that was why. And it wasn't even his fault!

The horses were out in the back field. There was grass out there, but she liked to make sure they had extra feed, especially now that Jake's horse was grazing, too. This was an acreage, not a full farm, so the actual grazing field wasn't as large as it could be for three horses.

Adel lifted a bale into a wheelbarrow, and it took her a few attempts to get it inside. A compressed bale of alfalfa hay was incredibly heavy, but she had a few tricks of her own to make the job easier. She started pushing the wheelbarrow toward the door, and the alfalfa tipped heavily to one side.

"Oh, no," she muttered, and she stopped, then grabbed the twine to readjust it.

"You want help?"

Adel looked up to see Jake standing in the doorway. He looked more impressive, somehow, backlit against the open entry. He was a tall, strong man... When she didn't immediately answer, he strode over, hoisted the bale up to get it balanced, then lifted the wheelbarrow by the handles.

"It's okay," Adel said, her voice suddenly coming back to her. "I can do it. We've been doing the work ourselves for years now."

"Come on, Adel," Jake said with a half smile. "What kind of man would I be watching a woman do the outdoor work while I ate peach pie inside?" He met her gaze, and didn't release the handles. "A lazy one, that's what. You can tell prospective matches that I at least know how to take care of men's work."

"I think your farm proves that," she replied, but she stepped back as he wheeled the hay out the door and toward the gate.

Adel jogged ahead and opened it, and he carried on through toward the big, iron feeder. This job always took most of Adel's strength, but he worked easily enough. He hoisted the bale up and over the side of the feeder, then pulled a pocketknife off a loop on his suspender. He popped the twine and the hay sprung free. The horses came ambling over to the new hay, and Jake walked back to the fence next to Adel, and leaned against the wooden rungs.

Adel looked over her shoulder toward the house. She could see her sister in the kitchen window, washing dishes.

"Jake, I think we need to talk about boundaries," Adel said.

"What kind?" he asked.

"The kind between a matchmaker and her client," she replied.

"Ah." He raised an eyebrow and waited.

"It's just that—" She swallowed. "I'm not your friend, or your schoolmate anymore. Things have changed. A lot has changed since you left. And you seem to be wanting to relate to me as a friend, and I can't be that right now."

"You can't be my friend." His tone was low, and he met her gaze easily enough.

"No." She straightened her shoulders. "I'm supposed to be your matchmaker, and in that role, I'm not the one you should be chatting with."

"So I should be chatting with Naomi?" he

asked. He looked back toward the house and waved. Naomi, in the window, waved back.

"If you want to," she replied.

"But not with you."

This wasn't going the way she intended, and she sighed. "Jake, I have limited time to find you a wife, and you're not cooperating."

"I'm being stubbornly personable and helpful come chore time," he said with a teasing little smile.

"Jake, cut it out! You know what I'm talking about, and you're purposefully misunderstanding me!"

"Maybe I am," he replied. "But you're being silly. I've known you since we were tiny. We used to stomp in puddles together in grade school. We had fun."

"I got into trouble for that," she said. "It was less fun for me. I'd go home with a filthy dress and my *mamm* would give me extra chores for being so careless."

"But while we were stomping, it was great!" He shot her a grin. "And there was that time we had to memorize that Christmas poem together."

"You didn't do it properly," she said. "You made us both look bad. I really cared about that Christmas presentation."

"I did try." Jake softened his tone. "I memorized and studied that poem for weeks. But I got nervous in front of people, and I forgot it all."

"You should have said that instead of making farm animal noises," she said. "You were a rebel from childhood, Jake."

Jake's joking disappeared. "I was ten. Ten-year-olds don't always deal with embarrassment gracefully. I could have run off in humiliation, or I could play it off like I meant to do it. I chose the latter."

His expression was serious now, and she felt her own cheeks warm.

"I didn't know you were embarrassed," she said.

"I'm not so bad in front of people now," he said. "But I still get a little nervous sometimes. And when I'm nervous, I…act like it's all part of the plan."

"Are you nervous now?" she asked.

"Yah."

"Well…don't be," she said. "I intend to find you a good wife. I want the best for you. I want to see you happy."

"You talk like you're some matronly aunt, or something, like you have no mutual history with me," he said. "We're the same age,

Adel. I'm not some young man looking to you for your wisdom. I'm your equal."

Adel sighed. "You're saying we have memories together. And you're right, but you're wasting your time using up your charm on *me*."

"Who else should I chat with?" He spread his arms and looked around. "And while I'm here, I'm supposed to act like a tourist or something? Eat your food and sit in my room? Eat the pie and watch you work? Would that make you more comfortable? I thought this was your idea—us getting to know each other so you'd be able to recommend me honestly. But I'm not going to pretend you're some old lady when you aren't!"

"I didn't say I was an old lady!" she shot back.

"Well, you're acting like one," he said.

Old? She was acting *old*? Annoyance surged up inside her.

"I'm acting like a respected member of this community who has been given the task of finding you a wife!"

"I think you're being fake," he replied.

"Me?" She tried to tamp down her rising anger. "How would you even know, Jake? You've been back for a few months, and I've chatted with you a few times. That's it. What do you know about who I am on a heart level? What do you know about what I've been through, and how I've contributed to this community?"

"Because you're scared of a human connection!" he retorted.

"I am not."

"This—" He waggled a finger between them. "This is a human connection. Seeing me as a man, as a whole and complete person, as your equal. That's a human connection. And it's freaking you out."

He caught her gaze and held it. Her heartbeat sped up and she broke off the eye contact and looked away. Yes, she was noticing the man in him, more than she should.

"This is too casual for a single man and woman to be together," she said. "You might recall that we do things differently here."

"We were friends once," he said.

"We were schoolmates. Not friends." It sounded harsh, but the distinction mattered. She felt bad all the same. "I don't mean for that to sound cruel, but we don't know each other as adults, Jake. We knew each other as *kinner*. It's different."

"Yah," he agreed, but he didn't look daunted,

either. "Very different. We're both all grown up now."

More than grown. She'd already buried a husband. And that wasn't an excuse—it was a fact. That love and loss had molded and changed her.

"But being grown and good-looking isn't everything, Jake," she said.

"Who are you calling good-looking?" he asked with a slow smile. "You or me?"

She'd said too much, and she felt her cheeks heat. "I'm not a vain woman—"

"So it's me?" He was teasing now, and she turned away.

"I normally have a little more poise than this."

"Then I take that as a compliment," he replied.

"You've been with the *Englishers* for too long," she said curtly.

He chuckled. "You're more human than you think, Adel." He was silent for a moment. "And for the record, you have matured into a beautiful woman."

And maybe Jake had been with *Englishers* too long, but there was something about Adel that he liked so much more on this side of thirty. She was serious, sure, but he sensed a softness under all that bravado. The things that enticed him in his younger years were no longer the same things he was looking for in a wife. And while he knew that Adel had zero interest in marriage right now, he did see what she had to offer—maturity, insight, grace, dignity. And it didn't hurt that she was also incredibly beautiful.

So yes, that last shred of immaturity in him was enjoying getting a reaction out of her. She might not want marriage, but she had noticed him, and he liked that.

"You shouldn't be flirting with me," Adel said.

"I know. I'm sorry. I didn't really mean to flirt. I was just being honest," he replied.

She cast him an unimpressed look. "You're supposed to be building a life. And a choice in wife is a very important one. You can't play with this."

"Who says I'm playing?" he countered. Then he sighed. "I'm sorry. I'm not going to tease you. You're right."

"This is serious," she said. "Because you have to build it from the ground up, and a marriage is part of the foundation. A life doesn't happen by accident. It is built one choice at a time. Every goal comes with a price. If you want to be a farmer, you have to buy the land. If you want to be a wood-worker, you have to be able to open a shop. And you can't do more than one thing, most times, because there is only so much time and so much money you can invest into it. When you marry, that choice is for a lifetime—the length of which, only *Gott* knows. So know-ing what you want and walking purposefully in that direction is incredibly important."

Jake nodded. "Did you do that—with your first marriage?"

"No." She smiled faintly. "I stumbled into a wonderful first marriage, and I can't take any credit for having done anything more than simply being a well-behaved girl who listened to her father about a man's character. But I've seen a lot since then, and I won't be simply stumbling into another marriage again."

Would any man live up to her ideals? he wondered.

"What if you stumbled into love?" he asked.

"That's an *Englisher* problem," she said. "Falling in love with the wrong person, I mean. For example, if a man is wonderful in many ways, but married to someone else, is it difficult for me to stop any inappropriate feelings for him? No. Not at all. It's the same with a man who isn't a good fit for my future. You don't stumble into love, Jake."

She was so serious, and she sounded so convincing that he was tempted to accept her word as unwavering truth, and yet he'd seen evidence to the contrary.

He smiled faintly. "I've heard of several people who have. Not with inappropriate people, but with someone they didn't expect."

"Then they weren't watching where they were walking," she replied.

That almost sounded like a challenge, but Adel wasn't looking to get married again, and she might very well get her wish if she was focused enough on keeping her single life. Sometimes people got what they prayed for, even if they later regretted it.

"*Englishers* wait for that experience—the tumbling into love," he said.

"And look at the success rate of those relationships!" she shot back. "I read in a paper a few years ago that their marriages fail at a tremendous rate. There isn't enough planning or serious thought put into it. There is a reason why we pursue marriages the way we do. Our young people get to have that experience...within boundaries. If they associate with appropriate friends, then they can trip into love wherever they like, as long as they behave appropriately in the process and get married. But when people come to a matchmaker, it is normally because that tactic didn't work, and they're ready to be more practical."

She raised her eyebrows at him, and he rolled his eyes.

"You have a point," he said. "We're no spring chickens, you and me."

Maybe he wouldn't be able to experience that falling into love after all.

"*You're* no spring chicken," she retorted. "I'm not available, so it doesn't matter."

Jake met her gaze, and they both laughed. Adel's face relaxed into a stunning smile. Some women grew more beautiful the older they got, and Adel was one of them. She really had no idea, did she?

"And speaking of choosing the right person to love, tomorrow morning, I'm going to bring you to visit a prospective wife," Adel said.

"Oh." Jake blinked. "Good. Who?"

"Lydia Speicher."

Jake combed his memory for some recollection of the woman, but he came up empty.

"She's in her late twenties right now," Adel said. "So she was a few years younger than us."

"Ah. I don't remember her at all."

"Then it will be a nice introduction," she replied. "We should get back."

As Jake walked next to Adel, he had to wonder how this was going to work. Would he feel anything special when he met the right woman? Or would it be completely practical—a choice based on age, relative good looks, cooking ability and a compatible personality?

Could he promise himself to a woman on those criteria alone?

Adel didn't like the idea of falling in love, but without some sort of tumble, what would a lifetime be like with the woman? Was learning to love a good woman enough?

That evening, Jake sat in the kitchen with a glass of lemonade in front of him. Adel had gone up to bed, and the kitchen was spotlessly clean. His mind was still running along similar lines as earlier that day—wondering if it would even be possible to choose a wife this quickly.

He'd heard some stories about some local

marriages. Ben Hochstetler had married an ex-Amish social worker who came to his farm to pick up an abandoned baby. He'd been stunned to hear that story! And then there was Thomas Weibe, who'd married Patience, the Amish schoolteacher who helped him out with his daughter. More shocking still, Thomas's brother Noah married the pregnant girl who was going to give her baby up for adoption to Thomas and Patience. How the family had sorted that one out, he still wasn't sure, but he'd been told the family stayed close. It would seem that the community of Redemption had seen its fair share of surprising and quick weddings… and all of them working out very nicely.

Maybe his wedding would join the ranks of the others, and he'd get both his farm and a woman he loved, too. The chances were very slim, but wasn't that where Gott worked best—when it seemed impossible?

The side door opened, and he looked up to see Naomi come inside with a flat of eggs balanced on one hand. She shot him a friendly smile.

"You're up still?" she said.

"So are you," he pointed out.

"I was just getting the egg order from the neighbor," she said. "We get them weekly."

Jake nodded. He wasn't sure what to say to that. Naomi brought the eggs to the counter and put them down, then glanced up the staircase.

"She's got her back up, hasn't she?" Naomi said.

"Well, she's staying very serious," he replied. "I have a feeling she sees me as a little boy sometimes."

"Oh, she comes across that way, but it's how she is when she's scared," Naomi replied.

"Of what?" he asked. "Me?"

"No…" Naomi poured herself a glass of lemonade and joined him at the table. "It's not you, exactly. The bishop gave her an incredibly tough job, you know."

"*Yah*, I know," he replied. "Marrying me off in two weeks. That's not easy."

"And if this task was given to anyone else, they'd do their best and their conscience would be clear," she said. "But for my sister, letting the bishop down isn't even an option."

"Why not?" he asked.

"Because the bishop is offering her a way forward that is hard to refuse. She's got a chance at being something more in this community—a leader of sorts. She's been through a lot, and she has advice she can give to others. She's respected, loved, and women go to her with their problems. You're a bit of a trial run for her."

"Oh…" He hadn't realized that. Was she having to prove herself with him?

"Adel and I are very different," Naomi said quietly. "What I wouldn't give for someone to need me."

She smiled wistfully, and Jake's stomach tightened. Was Naomi suggesting what he thought she was? She met his gaze, and then shook her head, laughing.

"You can relax, Jake. I'm not proposing marriage."

"You wouldn't be a bad choice," he said.

"I'd be a terrible choice," she replied. "I've seen the way you look at my sister."

Jake felt his face heat. "What do you mean?"

"You've noticed how gorgeous she is," Naomi said. "She's the only one who hasn't. She just gets prettier as the years go by. In fact, I think the two of you would be rather well matched."

"She doesn't want marriage again," Jake said. "And if I'm to get that farm in my name, I need a legal marriage right quick."

"Yes, there is that…" Naomi shrugged. "But you have a spark between you."

"I irritate her," he said with a low laugh.

"A little bit," Naomi admitted, and they both chuckled. "So are you really going to do this—scoop up a wife that fast?"

"Yah," he said, then hesitated. "I'll try. But I'm going to listen to my gut. Maybe I'll meet someone truly wonderful and know right away. Some men say that about their wives— they knew the moment they saw them."

"And what did you think the moment you saw Adel?" she asked with a grin.

"Naomi, you should be the matchmaker," he chuckled, waggling a finger at her.

"You can't take Adel so seriously," Naomi said. "She's a planner. When she and Mark couldn't have *kinner*, she was heartbroken, but she took solace in the idea that *Gott* had something else in mind that would make it all make sense. And then Mark died…" Naomi sighed. "My sister might have married Mark because he was kind and gentle and respected, and she wanted very badly to be a wife. But she fell deeply in love with him after the marriage. Without *kinner*, she was able to see the beauty in her life as his wife, even without babies. That's how much she loved him. So when he died, it was like all the beauty in her world winked out. You see her now—fresh, pretty, and eyes that sparkle? Well, she was a shell of herself. She was pale, thin, gaunt. She looked like she might die of heartbreak."

Jake leaned back in his chair, his gaze moving toward the staircase. How much had she endured that he hadn't given her credit for? He wished she'd been the one to tell him this, instead of her sister.

"She found a way to embrace all that loss," Naomi went on, "and it was by holding on to Mark's memory. She's the deacon's widow, and there is still a role for her in this community in that capacity. It not only gives her a future where she can contribute in a meaningful way, but it means that everything she lost came together into something good."

"And if she married, it would negate it all… in a way. For her, at least," he concluded.

"Yah." Naomi nodded. "Exactly."

"I should stop teasing her," he said softly.

"No!" Naomi shook her head. "Not at all! She laughs with you. You get a rise out of her. You're reminding her that she's not the old woman she wishes she was! She has a whole life ahead of her, and I think it's good if you jostle her out of her comfortable rut."

"But you said—" he started.

"Compassion is a good thing," Naomi said. "But my sister needs to live, too. Not just grieve all the time. Sometimes, we go through hard times and there is no explanation why. It's a different kind of faith that keeps on believing *Gott* is good and life is good, too, in the face of that."

Why was Naomi telling him all of this? It was very personal information, and with the way he'd been joking with Adel and teasing her, he thought her sister might want him to let up. So why was she divulging this if she wasn't wanting him to leave Adel alone?

"You want to see her married again," Jake guessed.

"I truly do." Naomi smiled. "And you'd do nicely as a brother-in-law."

He laughed and shook his head. "I think it'll take some time to get your sister married again, especially after all you've told me. And time is not on my side."

Naomi nodded. "Very likely." She rose to her feet and drained the glass of lemonade. "I'd better turn in. I have a busy day tomorrow. We have two tourist groups coming through."

"Good night," he said. "And thank you for the explanation."

Even if he didn't really deserve all that information, it was nice to know. It made Adel make a little more sense to him.

"I'm praying you find a wonderful wife, Jake," Naomi said.

"Thank you." He smiled. "I appreciate that."

Naomi headed up the stairs, and Jake stayed where he was, the clock on the wall ticking comfortingly in the background. Adel was beautiful, interesting, and she'd definitely caught his attention. But she wasn't ready for marriage again, and with her sister's explanation, he could fully understand why. If only he weren't on this unfair time constraint, and he could take his time and get to know her better.

But that wasn't the way things were. If he was going to keep this farm, he needed a wife in a matter of days. And perhaps that was *Gott*'s intention, forcing him to move on and look further for a wife. Maybe this Lydia Speicher would be the one for him. Who knew? *Gott* could move very quickly when He wanted to.

Gott, *show me the woman for me,* Jake prayed. *And when You do, make it very clear.*

Because I don't think my head is on straight right now.

It couldn't be if he was feeling this way about his matchmaker!

Chapter Five

Adel had chosen Lydia Speicher for a reason. Lydia was a kind woman, but she was strong, too. Redemption had a good number of strong, self-sufficient women. To run an Amish home took a great deal of skill and fortitude, and the woman who married Jake would need every last ounce just to put that home back together again.

Lydia was twenty-eight, and somehow, she'd just never been courted. It happened sometimes—a girl would have too much competition, or just not enough boys her age, and she'd end up left behind when everyone else was getting married and setting up their own homes.

Adel had suggested that Lydia go visit some friends in another community, and she hadn't had any luck there, either. So when Adel said she might have someone for her, Lydia had enthusiastically agreed to meet him.

Jake held the reins loosely in his hands, and he leaned forward to check traffic before he flicked them and the buggy started forward. A car whipped past them, and Adel reached out and grabbed Jake's sleeve. He cast her an amused smile.

"I'm fine," he said. "I've driven both cars and buggies."

She let out a breath. "*Yah*, I know."

His gaze flickered toward her again. "You're used to being the one holding the reins. That's what this is."

Adel felt her cheeks heat. "I might be used to it, *yah*."

It had been five years of fending for herself, and she'd started to even enjoy taking care of things herself. It drove Naomi crazy. She said Adel had gotten bossy.

"Do you want to drive?" he asked.

"No! It would look very bad for me to drive you to see a woman about marriage. You'd look—" She saw the twinkle in his eye. "You were joking."

"I was joking." He chuckled. "Lean back

and stop mentally driving this buggy, Adel. I can get us to the Speichers' farm."

Adel let out a breath. He was right, of course. She was trying to do everything herself again. No doubt, Naomi would be able to joke with Jake endlessly about Adel's tendency to do that.

"I never did ask, does Lydia remember me?" Jake asked.

"She does, actually," Adel replied. She repressed the urge to point out that the next intersection ahead was where Jake needed to take a right-hand turn.

"Is that a good thing or a bad thing?" he asked.

"She remembers you being a rather rebellious older boy," Adel said. "But she thought you were handsome back then, and if you've gotten over the rebellious bit, she'd be very happy to meet you again."

"What did you tell her?" he asked.

"That you've chosen an Amish life," she said.

"That's it?"

"And that I think you'll stay Amish," she said. "You might always be a little rebellious, though."

"That's fair." He reined in the horse at the

next intersection, and flicked the battery-operated turn signal. "If she'll still see me after that explanation, then we might have a chance."

Adel tried to tamp down the twinge of discomfort she felt. It wasn't that she thought the two wouldn't be a good match. She wouldn't have suggested it otherwise. It was something else…the tiniest swell of jealousy. What was wrong with her?

"You do know the way," Adel said as he brought the buggy around the corner.

"Of course," he replied with a chuckle. "I've been back for months, Adel."

The Speicher drive was half a mile down the road and their name was on the mailbox. As they pulled in, Adel felt a flutter in her stomach. This was it—her first matchmaker introduction. She'd have to stop this foolishness she was feeling for Jake, and make sure she presented herself properly. This very well might be the beginning of an important role in this community.

The side door opened as they pulled up next to the house, and Bonita Speicher, Lydia's mother, appeared on the step.

"Hello!" Adel called cheerily.

Bonita waved and smiled. Jake led the

horse up to a water bucket, let him drink and then strapped on a feed bag. They walked together up to the house, and Bonita stood back to let them inside.

For the first few minutes, there were the general introductions. Bonita said that she remembered Jake from boyhood, and she'd actually had a pleasant memory of him—cutting the lawn here when her husband had a broken leg. Lydia stood by the sink looking bashful, and then she came forward and shook his hand.

"Hello," Lydia said.

There was an assortment of baked goods on plates on the table—very likely all made by Lydia's hand. Lydia invited Jake to sit down, and Adel and Bonita retreated to the other side of the kitchen.

"What do you think of him?" Bonita asked, her voice low. "Honestly?"

"He's a good man," Adel replied. "I wouldn't have brought him by otherwise."

"He never did like the rules," Bonita said. "And now we find out he came back because of the will."

"He always did want to return," Adel said. "He just didn't know how. It isn't my story to tell, but… It was more complicated."

Bonita nodded. "My daughter likes him. You can tell by the way she's feeding him."

Adel looked over to see Bonita pushing a plate of cookies in Jake's direction. Jake took one and gave her a polite nod. They watched the couple in silence for a couple of beats.

"This is where I make the case for my daughter," Bonita said. "She's smart, she's a wonderful cook and she takes after my mother, who is still doing her own laundry and gardening at eighty-seven. She's got a good heart, and she'd given up on finding a husband. I'd love to see her married."

"You don't have to make your case to me," Adel said. "Lydia is wonderful."

"She's a little stubborn, too..." Bonita blushed.

"A good thing in this situation," Adel said. "If they hit it off, there will be a lot of learning between the two of them. He'll need a strong woman."

Bonita exhaled. "*Yah*... Well, let's go join them now."

Bonita led the way, and Adel followed. They pulled up some chairs, and Adel met Jake's gaze. He pressed his lips together.

"So what work did you do when you were... over the fence?" Lydia asked.

"I worked at a factory," he replied. "It was pretty good pay, and I liked my coworkers a lot."

"Oh…" Lydia glanced over at Adel, looking mildly panicked. Had they run out of things to talk about already?

"Jake is working to put his uncle's farm back together again," Adel supplied. "He's quite passionate about the barn roof."

"Are you?" Lydia asked.

"Uh—" Jake nodded. "Maybe not passionate so much as wanting to replace it. The barn is in pretty good shape. It's a strong building, but it won't stay that way with all the leaking going on. The supports will rot."

"True," Lydia said. "When will you do it?"

"When it's mine," he said. "I've put a lot of time and effort into fixing things up, but I can't put any more personal money into it if it won't be mine. Whoever owns that land will replace the roof. I'm just hoping it's me."

"And the house?" Lydia asked. "How is it?"

Jake's cheeks reddened a little bit. "It's… in need of work."

"Hmm." Lydia wouldn't ask too much about it, or it would look like all she cared about was the farm.

"Lydia won a quilting contest at the fair," Adel said. "She's very skilled with a needle."

"Nice!" Jake smiled. "Congratulations. You must like quilting, then?"

"I like crocheting more," she said.

Jake fell silent. This was getting very awkward. Adel reached out with her foot under the table and gave Jake's boot a nudge. He looked over at her, surprise on his face, then he smiled.

"Do you want to show me something you've crocheted? Honestly, I've never learned much about it. My *mamm*—" He swallowed. "She didn't crochet much. She did more sewing. That I can remember, at least."

"Of course I'll show you." Lydia pushed back her chair. "You don't seem hungry."

"I'm kind of nervous," he replied.

"The spare room upstairs has become a sewing room," Lydia said. "Come up with me, and I'll show you what I've been doing."

Bonita cast Adel a questioning look and Adel shrugged.

"They're both adults," Adel said softly as the two disappeared up the stairs. "And well-behaved adults, too. Trust me, Jake is looking for a wife. Listen."

The soft murmur of their voices came

down the staircase, and then through the ceiling from above. Adel found herself straining to make out words, but she couldn't.

"How is it that you're acting as matchmaker for Jacob Knussli?" Bonita asked. She nudged a plate of cookies toward Adel, and she took one. It was a buttery shortbread, and she chewed and swallowed before answering.

"The bishop asked me," she said. "I was surprised, too, but honestly, Bonita? I'd love to do more of this."

"You should be finding yourself a match," Bonita said with a wink. "You're very young, you know."

"Oh…" Adel shrugged. "I don't know about that. I'm not looking for a husband."

"Well, I'm glad you're thinking about getting our young people married. Definitely keep my daughter in mind, even if this match doesn't work."

There was something in Bonita's voice that made Adel give her a questioning look.

"You think it won't work?" Adel said. "Give them some time. They have to break the ice."

"The most relaxed that man ever looked was when he was looking at you," Bonita said. That was similar to what her sister had told her about the way Jake gazed at her. She might need to warn him that he'd best stop that, or he'd come across as interested in the wrong woman.

"He's nervous," Adel said. "This is a big step—getting to know a woman in hopes of marrying her that quickly. Of course, he's not at his best. In fact, he's normally quite charming. He chats for hours. I think it's a good sign if he's a bit nervous with her."

Bonita gave her a funny look, but didn't say anything.

The floorboards overhead squeaked, and Jake's boots could be heard on the staircase coming down.

"It was so nice to meet you," Jake was saying. "Properly, I mean. Thank you for the tour."

Jake and Lydia came back down into the kitchen, and Lydia was looking at Jake uncertainly. Jake looked over at Adel and met her gaze meaningfully. He was ready to go, it would seem.

"Well—" Adel forced a smile. "We'll be in touch, and everyone can talk and see how they feel…" Adel shot Lydia a smile. "Your baking is amazing, Lydia. I know if I ask for the recipe, I'll never be able to repeat it."

"Oh, you're too kind," Lydia said with a blush, but she did grab a paper bag from a drawer, and she filled it with baked goods. "For the drive home." She handed it to Jake.

"Thank you. I do appreciate it." He held the bag in both hands. "Goodbye. So nice to see you, too." He gave Bonita a smile.

After a few more cordial farewells, Adel followed Jake out to the buggy. He walked faster than her, and while she boosted herself up into the seat, he saw to the horse's feed bag. When he joined her, he dropped the paper bag between them. Adel leaned forward and waved to Bonita and Lydia, who both stood on the step side by side.

Jake flicked the reins and turned the buggy around. He exhaled a slow breath as they rattled up the drive toward the road.

"So…" Adel felt a little tightening in her chest. "What did you think of Lydia?"

Jake leaned back as the buggy rattled up onto the main road, and he let out a slow breath. It was a relief to be driving away, and every yard the buggy moved, the better he felt. There was absolutely nothing wrong with that family. They were good Amish people, and the home had been immaculately kept. The baked goods in the bag next to him were going to be absolutely delicious if he could relax enough to actually eat them. He was looking for a wife, and Lydia was painfully appropriate.

He looked over to find Adel's gaze locked on his face.

"Uh—" He swallowed. "She's a lovely person."

"She is," Adel agreed. "I wouldn't have brought you otherwise."

He nodded. "And she's very nice."

"Oh, Jake, now is not the time for politeness!" Adel said. "I won't give a word-for-word report back to anyone. As your matchmaker, I need to know your honest thoughts. Could you make a life with her?"

Could he? He tried to imagine coming back to his farmhouse and finding Lydia inside. There would be delicious cooking, he was absolutely sure. The house would be clean like the one they'd just left. And Lydia would be there waiting for him in her neat cape dress and crisp white apron. Lydia. A very nice woman.

"I probably could…" Jake sighed. "She's a good cook. She's moderately attractive. She seems to be good with crochet and quilting. If she got her hands onto a house, it would be put in order in no time."

Adel nodded. "Yes, a very good point. She'd

be good with needlework and she knits some really beautiful blankets, too."

As if he cared about the intricacy of her needlework, or the quality of the lap blankets. Maybe he should care about those things a bit more, but he didn't. Jake needed to be reasonable here. He was looking for a good woman to marry in a ridiculously short amount of time. And Lydia checked all the boxes but one.

"Her mother remembered you from when you helped cut their grass when her husband was injured," Adel said. "And they'd accept a quick marriage for their daughter. They're a very nice family, if you recall."

"Their son is Mordecai Speicher, right?" he said.

"*Yah*—he was in our grade."

"I didn't like him much…"

He could almost hear Adel rolling her eyes beside him. And he knew he was grasping at excuses here.

"What's wrong with her brother?" Adel asked. "He owns a trinket shop in town. He does quite well, actually."

"He was always kind of pompous," he replied. "I don't know. I didn't like him. That's all."

"Are you telling me that he's an obstacle

for you?" Adel asked. "Would you like to see him again and see if you could manage being related to him? I'm sure I could set up a visit."

"No, no," he said with a shake of his head. "That's not necessary."

"Do you want to know what I think?" Adel asked.

He looked over at her, a sense of relief flooding through him. If this was left to his feelings, he wasn't going to know the right step. But someone with some perspective would be incredibly helpful. That was what matchmakers were for, wasn't it?

"Yes," he said. "I really do."

"I think she's strong enough to keep you in line," she said.

Jake met her gaze, and then laughed. "Are you serious?"

"Deadly," she replied. "She's very strong in the faith, and she knows right from wrong. She also doesn't take any guff. I think she'd be good for you."

"So... You think I need that?" he asked. "Is that a real worry here?"

Adel cast him a wry smile. "You're a rebel, Jake. Rebels need someone who stands up to them. Lydia would do that."

"I think you stand up to me just fine," he said.

"I do," she said. "Because I'm not cowed by your charm or good looks. But I'm not going to be around day in and day out to keep you in line, am I?"

Jake chuckled. "Okay... So opposites can be good for each other."

They rode in silence for a few minutes, and Jake wondered if he was being too picky. Lydia was a very nice woman, and besides one obnoxious brother, she came from a very nice family. He was the one looking for a wife, so what was his problem here?

"So what's the matter?" Adel asked, mirroring his thoughts.

Jake reined the horse in at the four-way stop, then proceeded around the corner, a little faster than usual, Adel was jostled against him as the wheel hit a rock in the road, and her warm arm pressed into his side. He put a hand out instinctively and caught her fingers in his.

His heartbeat sped up, and for one eternal moment, her hand clasped in his, he felt a tug toward her so strong that it shocked him. No! This wasn't the woman who was available. Was this just some way of sabotaging himself?

He let go of her hand and when he allowed

himself to glance at her face, the stern stare was gone, and she was looking at him questioningly. Great. He'd seem foolish if she knew what he'd just been thinking.

"We need to nail this down so I know how to proceed," Adel said.

With Lydia. Right.

"I don't think she's the one for me," he said. "I mean, she's perfectly pleasant, talented, nice-looking…"

He glanced over at Adel. But Lydia wasn't as beautiful as this woman beside him. And he couldn't bring himself to open up with Lydia—not naturally. He'd felt quite open with Adel from their first meeting—even with Adel doing her best to keep him at arm's length. And that ability seemed rather important in a marriage.

"What?" Adel asked.

"I think Lydia deserves a man who thinks she's wonderful," Jake said. "She deserves a man who wants to steal a kiss with her."

"The kisses would come in time," Adel said.

"You think?" He wasn't convinced of that.

"I've been married," Adel said gently.

"And I haven't, so you're the expert here," he admitted.

"At first, I was shy and uncertain, and then one day, about a week after our wedding, things just relaxed with us. It does take a little bit of time, Jake. No one goes from modest discretion to marriage without a little bit of transition."

"Don't they?" he asked.

She shook her head. "Nope. The first year of marriage is all about adjusting. And that adjustment looks different for every couple."

But he was assuming that the grooms in these marriages at least wanted to kiss their wives. As nice as Lydia was, he couldn't imagine kissing her.

"It's just that I don't feel any kind of spark with her," he confessed. "Like…any spark at all. I don't think anything would suddenly ignite a week after the wedding like it did for you. You fell deeply in love, Adel. It took you some time, but that was real, honest love."

She froze, and he realized his mistake the moment it was out of his mouth. Adel hadn't told him that. Her sister had. He looked over at her and winced.

"Naomi told me that," he said.

Adel sighed. "Did she, now."

He could hear the annoyance in her tone, and he couldn't help but grin at her.

"Your sister knows you, Adel. Be glad of that."

"She doesn't need to make sure you know me just as well as she does," Adel retorted. "I'm your matchmaker, not your match!"

True. If Adel was his match, it might be easier. He could imagine kissing Adel, and he could imagine enjoying it very much. He felt his face heat, and he pulled his mind away from the brink.

"The point remains," Jake said, "there was something really special between you and Mark. And I don't feel that with Lydia. I don't even feel the beginning of that..."

Adel nodded. "That's fine. It's good to know that there isn't something specific that's wrong. If it's a matter of a spark, maybe my next introduction will be more successful. Do you want to go meet her now?"

"Not really," he said with a faint smile. "I think I just need to unwind a while before I meet the next one."

"That's fair," Adel said, and she suddenly broke into a stunning smile. "You look downright terrified, Jake."

"That's amusing?" he muttered.

"It's a relief," she said. "I hope you're

scared—at least a little bit. It means you're finally seeing how serious this choice is."

He saw the sign for the bed-and-breakfast approaching. If only he had more time, or the days could stretch just a little bit longer as he got his balance.

Wife hunting was turning out to be the most stressful thing he'd done in his life.

Chapter Six

When Adel got back into the house, the kitchen was clean, and it still smelled of vegetable soup from the tourist groups who came through. They always served a delicious soup with crusty bread and butter from the Petersheim Creamery that made the most delicious butter blends in Pennsylvania. A note lay on the counter in her sister's familiar handwriting.

Both tourist groups have come and gone. They went well! Dishes are done—as you can see. Ha, ha! I'm going to help Maria with her garden for a couple of hours, and I'll stop by the creamery for our butter order. You don't mind starting dinner, do you?

There was no signature at the bottom, and there didn't need to be. It was just as well that her sister had gone out. Adel's mind was still on the introduction with Lydia. It would seem that Jake was truly not interested in pursuing more with Lydia, but maybe she should hold off on telling Lydia that for a few days. Perhaps he'd circle back around later, after some time to think.

Being a matchmaker sounded lovely when it came to finding marriage matches for people, but she wasn't looking forward to telling the ones who weren't chosen the bad news. What could she tell Lydia—that Jake simply didn't feel a connection? Granted, it could go the other direction, and a woman who did interest Jake might not be interested in return. The path to love was fraught with disappointment, and she would be not only the bearer of good news, but of bad, as well.

And then there was the unsettling fact that she was actually feeling relieved that this introduction hadn't worked. What did this say about her? She'd been so certain that she was ready to step into the role of matchmaker, and when faced with a handsome man in want of a wife, she was feeling jealous of the women who might interest him?

Gott, *wash my heart out,* she prayed. *I want You to use me, and I'm being petty! Help me to stop feeling this way. It isn't about me, and I know that.*

She pulled a chicken out of the icebox and deposited it into a roasting pan just as the side door opened. Jake came into the kitchen and he glanced around.

"I gave the horses the extra feed a bit early. I hope you don't mind."

"No, I appreciate it. Thank you." He didn't have to do that, but it was sweet of him to insist. She went to the windowsill where she grew some herbs and plucked some twigs of thyme and parsley.

"Chicken dinner tonight?" Jake asked.

"Yah." She cast him a smile. "I thought we could all use a comforting meal."

"Do I seem a little shaken?" he asked, but she heard humor in his tone.

"A little bit," she admitted. "Tomorrow morning, we have another appointment. This one is with Delia Swarey."

"Delia… She was married to Zeke Swarey for years," he said.

"He passed away," she replied. "Two years ago. He got lung cancer."

"I didn't hear about that." He sighed. "That's too bad. And she's looking for a new husband?"

"She's ready to consider it, *yah*," Adel replied.

"She's older than us, though," he said.

"By two years. At this point in life, it doesn't matter as much. She's got the four boys to raise on her own, and they need a *daet*."

"How old are they?" he asked.

"Between twelve and seventeen." They were good boys, but they were strong-willed, and Delia had been struggling with raising them alone. Parenting was one part of life that Adel couldn't give advice on, but she knew that the bishop had visited Delia's home to talk to the boys about some infraction or other.

"And you thought I'd be a good father?" Jake asked.

"I thought you could grow into the role," she replied. "Like every man does."

"I wouldn't be starting with babies," he said. "That's how most fathers start, and they learn as they go. They aren't starting with teens."

Adel regarded him for a moment, and he was right. She knew exactly what she was suggesting when she put Delia's name on her list. Jake was a strong man who'd seen the world already. His experiences could be valuable to some equally rebellious stepsons who might be saved some hard lessons of their own. Besides, it was good to be needed—and challenged—in a relationship.

"Perhaps I have faith in you," she said.

Jake's expression changed to something more self-conscious, and he lifted his shoulders. "Thank you. You really think I could handle it?"

"I do," she replied. "You can handle a lot more than you think. We don't grow into our true full potential comfortably, you know."

"You're probably right." He nodded toward the bag of potatoes on the counter. "Why don't I give you a hand?"

He didn't wait for her to answer, and he pulled open a couple of drawers at random, and pulled out a peeler. Adel watched him in mute surprise. Help in the kitchen? *Why?*

"Do you have a bucket to peel into?" he asked. "Oh, here it is."

He grabbed an old ice cream pail used for food bits that would be sent out to compost.

"What are you doing?" she asked. "You're my guest here, and helping with the animals is more than enough. I provide meals. You don't need to—"

"I'm a good cook," he said, one side of his mouth turning up in a half smile.

Was this a comment about her cooking? She

wasn't entirely sure. She'd never seen a man volunteer to help in the kitchen over the age of twelve. *Kinner* helped their *mamms*, but grown men sat themselves down and waited. Their work was payment enough, and they knew it.

"This isn't a man's job," she said pointedly. "Go sit down. I'll take care of this."

"You know, the *Englisher* men cook," he said. "And in my time away, I've learned. It was either that, or starve. And I like tasty food. I'm pretty sure my mashed potatoes would rival even yours."

Adel laughed uncomfortably. "You can't be serious, Jake."

Her mashed potatoes were a fluffy, buttery delight. Guests Amish and English alike always complimented her on her perfect mashed potatoes.

"I'm completely serious," he replied. "I need butter, some cream cheese, black pepper and maybe a bit of cheddar, if you have it."

She glanced toward the icebox. "I actually have all of that…"

"Excellent. Prepare to be impressed."

"Amish men leave the cooking to the women," Adel said. "You know that."

Jake ignored her and started peeling potatoes. He worked quickly, his hands seeming to know the work as the peels curled and dropped into the bucket. His hands were strong and work-worn, and she found her eyes drawn to his strong forearms as he peeled.

"This will not impress the women I set you up with," she said. "They're looking for an Amish husband. Whatever you picked up with the English is best left there, you know."

"I'm not trying to impress them," he said, looking up for the first time. His dark gaze locked onto hers meaningfully, and her breath caught. He didn't drop his gaze, either, and she felt her pulse speeding up. "This is about me just being me. And tonight, I want to cook with you."

He dropped his gaze then and turned back to his work. She exhaled a pent-up a breath, and her face felt hot. Was she blushing? She put her fingers against her cheeks. If Jake had used a bit of that smolder on Lydia, today's introduction might have gone better...

"So you like cooking?" she asked, her voice sounding strange in her own ears.

"*Yah.* It's relaxing. I enjoy it. I get to make food the way I like it."

"Oh..."

"I don't mean that as an insult to your good cooking, Adel," he said, his voice softening.

"I could grow plenty fat just eating what you put out, I assure you."

"Thank you… I think." She chuckled.

"I've obviously got a lot on my mind, and sitting there watching you cook isn't going to help," he said. "I'm antsy. And I'll go back to my own farm and get to work soon enough, but until I do, I'd rather have your company than not."

Adel felt the compliment in his words, and she turned back to trimming the chicken. "It's nice to have the company…other than my sister. Although this does feel strange to be cooking with a man."

"If it isn't strange to do dishes with a man, why would it be strange to cook with one?" he asked. "Where are your knives?"

"You're standing in front of the drawer."

"Thanks." He pulled out a paring knife and cut the few potatoes he'd already peeled, then picked up a fresh potato and the peeler once more. "You tell me when to stop peeling. I'm used to cooking for one."

She looked over his arm at the potatoes in the pot. "Keep going."

She added the fresh herbs and a few dried ones to the chicken, then poured some water into the pan. A roasted chicken almost cooked itself, she always said. She grabbed an onion out of a bowl on the counter and reached for a cutting board.

"Who taught you to cook?" she asked.

"TV." He shrugged. "They have these cooking shows where you watch people make meals, and I figured out the basics that way."

"Wow... That's so different," she said. "I honestly thought you'd say a woman taught you."

"Well, she was a woman, but she was on TV." He shot her a teasing smile.

"And you weren't trying to impress an *Englisher* with all this?" she asked.

"No, I just wanted to eat," he replied. "Now, tonight, there is the smallest chance I'm trying to impress you."

Adel rolled her eyes. "I told you that Amish women aren't impressed by this."

"Most Amish women probably aren't." He leaned over and nudged her arm with his elbow. "But you are...just a bit. You can admit it."

Adel laughed, and when she looked up at him, his eyes glittered with humor.

"A little bit," she admitted. "But you'd shock every available woman in Redemption."

"Then by all means, keep this to yourself," he replied with a grin.

Adel continued to chop onions and celery,

dumped them into the pan with the water and the chicken, drizzled some oil over the whole lot, and then went to the big, black wood-burning stove and squatted down to add some wood to the fire.

"Would you mind cranking open that window a little farther?" she asked.

Jake did as she asked, and she put another couple of logs into the fire, then closed the door. Jake put his pot onto the stove, and he held out his hand as she started to rise. Without thinking, she accepted, and he boosted her easily to her feet. But once standing, she found herself so close to him that her dress brushed the front of his pants.

Jake didn't release her hand, and she didn't move. It was like the room melted away, and it was just this man, the musky scent of him, his strong fingers holding her up.

It had been a very long time since Adel had been in a room alone with a man, let alone one as handsome as Jake was. It had been even longer since a man had held her hand like this… Because this was something different than a hand shake or simple assistance. This made her breath come quick and her knees feel weak. She licked her lips and pulled back her hand.

"I should get started on the salad," she said, just a little bit louder than she needed to. It felt like she'd almost shouted into his face, and she felt her face heat with embarrassment again. She really did have more decorum than this with other people!

"*Yah.* Sure." He hesitated for a beat, and then he stepped back. "Maybe I'll just get a drink of water."

They parted ways, and Adel couldn't help but steal a look over her shoulder as he filled a water glass from the tap. He was tall, and so well built. It was a scandalous thing to even notice, but there was something about Jake that kept tapping on a door inside her heart that she'd closed very firmly at her husband's death. And the embarrassing part was, he seemed to do it without even noticing, or trying. What did that say about her? Why on earth did the good bishop choose her to find Jake Knussli a wife? The bishop should have chosen an older woman with wisdom, and wrinkles, one who wouldn't be swayed by this man's charm.

But then, how could the bishop have possibly known that the likes of Jake Knussli would sway her? This was her own humbling truth to bear.

* * *

Jake drained a glass of water at the sink, and his heart was beating just a bit faster than it should be. Adel was a truly beautiful woman, and standing next to her at the stove had brought some heat to his face that had nothing to do with the stove next to them. She was more than beautiful—she was interesting, and deep, and wise, and… Was there a word to describe the way he felt himself pulled toward her, like he was caught in a current?

Jake watched as she rinsed lettuce at the sink, refusing to look at him as she worked. Had he made things weird between them now? Maybe there was a rebellious streak in him still, because he knew he was knocking her off her balance by offering to cook. He knew this wasn't the traditional Amish way, and yet he was doing it. Why? To be true to his own way of doing things? That shouldn't matter with his matchmaker, should it?

If he had to be completely honest with himself, he liked getting a reaction out of *her*. It wasn't that he wanted to prove he was so different, so much as he wanted to show her who he really was deep down. This was going to prove a problem.

"Are you sure you want to be Amish?" Adel asked, and it pulled Jake out of his thoughts.

"What?" he asked.

"You haven't come back all the way," she said.

"I'm here," he replied. "That counts."

"You haven't left behind all of your *Englisher* ways, either," she countered.

Jake met her gaze for a moment. "Life changes a person. My life certainly formed me, and that isn't a bad thing. I can't strip away fifteen years of maturing in order to come back to an Amish core. And I don't think you'd really want that. I grew in a lot of ways out there. I learned to cook. I also learned to appreciate everything I'd left behind. I'm going to be a combination of all of it—my Amish upbringing and my English experiences. It's the choice to live Amish that should matter."

She didn't answer, and he wondered if she disagreed.

"If a young married couple is living alone, and the wife is pregnant," Jake said, "and let's say that she gets sick and can't cook for a few days, would the Amish husband cook?"

"Of course," she replied.

"And if an Amish wife got sick with a flu,

the husband would prepare the meals for the *kinner*," he said.

"Those are emergencies," she said.

"Those are expressions of love." She froze, and as the words came out, he knew how it sounded. "What I mean is, it doesn't have to be a dire emergency for a man to cook. He might be doing it because he cares. Or because he enjoys it. Or because he enjoys a woman's company…"

He was being too honest. What was he doing?

"Do you—" She didn't look up from the cutting board, her fingers working quickly as she chopped. "Do you really like my company?"

The chopping stopped then, and she didn't turn. She cared about his answer—he could tell. He swallowed.

"*Yah*, I… I do like your company. Better than anyone else I've met so far."

His heartbeat hammered in his throat. Adel looked at him over her shoulder, and she smiled.

"You're just saying that," she said.

"Adel, I'm not asking for anything," he said. "I know where you stand. I'm just saying that I'm more comfortable with you somehow. I can be myself, and you can chide me for it, and you're still someone I like to be with."

"You should try harder to like the available women," she said.

"I am trying," he replied. "I know exactly what's on the line here. But it's fully possible for us to be friends, you know."

"Friends?" She smiled faintly. "You'll be a married man, if all goes according to plan."

"Well, until I'm a married man, then," he said.

"And how is that fair to me?" she retorted. "We spend time together, we get to know each other, to enjoy each other's company, and then you whisk off to married life. Just as you should! But it's not very fair to the friend left behind who can't continue being your friend in that way, is it?"

"Maybe not," he agreed. "Are you saying you'll miss me?"

Her cheeks colored. "I'm your matchmaker."

"And you *like* me." He shot her a grin. "I'm fun. I cook. Just wait until you taste those mashed potatoes."

Teasing her was easier somehow. When he was joking around, he could say what he meant, and what he felt, and he didn't feel foolish. Because if he dropped the joking, he'd just have to say what he felt, and that couldn't end well.

The potatoes were boiling on the stove, and he went over to check them. He used an oven mitt to lift the lid on the pot, and stabbed them with a fork. They were soft enough now. The kitchen had begun to smell pleasantly of roasting chicken.

Jake drained the potatoes into the sink, then he headed to the icebox and pulled out butter, cream cheese and a little block of cheddar.

"I just need a—" he started, and she held out a potato masher. "Thanks."

They exchanged an amused smile, and she crossed her arms and leaned against the counter, watching him. He didn't normally cook with this much direct attention, but with her, he didn't mind.

"Now, it's all about the cream-cheese-to-chive balance," he said.

"I'll mince some chives for you. How much?"

"About…" He didn't normally measure. "Oh, a handful, I suppose."

Adel chuckled. "You're that kind of cook, are you?"

"Hey, my skill is all about instinct," he joked. "Not recipes."

As he mashed potatoes and added ingredients, he listened to the soft tap of Adel's knife chopping chives. Then she appeared at his elbow with a small bowl of the minced herbs.

"Enough?" she asked.

"Perfect." He dumped the chives into the potatoes and continued to mash. Then he added the cream cheese, then the cheddar, a lump of butter, a dash of salt… When he was satisfied with the consistency, he picked up the fork from the counter and lifted a bite to her lips. "Taste it for me."

Adel looked surprised, and she parted her lips and he slid the bite of mashed potatoes into her mouth. She took the fork from his fingers and pulled it slowly out from between her lips.

"Jake, this is amazing," she said, swallowing.

He felt a little surge of pride. "Thanks."

"No, I mean, really, really good." She looked into the pot and inhaled deeply.

"So you're impressed?" He met her gaze teasingly, but deep down, he wanted to know.

"I'm impressed, Jacob. You can cook."

He grinned. "That's what I needed to hear."

Why he'd needed that confirmation from her, he wasn't quite sure. But he did care about her opinion, even if he never got to cook at home with whatever woman he married. And the thought of marriage to some faceless woman suddenly felt heavy and uncomfortable. This state was easier—single, looking and with plenty of reason to spend time with Adel.

He heard footsteps on the stairs outside, and then the side door opened. Naomi came inside, her curls erupting from her *kapp* like a ginger explosion. She was carrying a plastic bag in one hand, and her cheeks were reddened from the heat.

"Hello," Naomi said hesitantly.

Suddenly, Jake was very aware of how close he and Adel were standing to each other. Her arm brushed against his, and if he just reached out, he could have easily slid his hand around her waist. Naomi's gaze flickered quickly between them.

"You're back." Adel took a step away from him, and her voice sounded slightly breathy. "Jake here made the mashed potatoes."

"Why?" Naomi asked.

"Because I wanted to!" he replied with a short laugh. "And they're good."

He looked down at Adel and she glanced up at the same time. She smiled—a sweet smile, just for him—and said, "They really are good."

"Did you tell Lydia that you like kitchen work?" Naomi asked.

Both women looked at him then, and Jake rolled his eyes. "No, I didn't. Naomi, is this really so shocking?"

"It's…unusual," Naomi said. "Nothing I'd brag about, Jake."

"So it's going to be a problem finding a woman who'll let me make my mashed potatoes?" he asked with a laugh.

"It'll be a challenge finding a woman who lets you anywhere near her kitchen if she thinks you're going to meddle with the meal," Naomi said with a chuckle. "Let me try those potatoes."

She got a fork from the drawer and Jake stepped back as both women leaned over the pot. Naomi took a bite, exchanged a wide-eyed look with her sister and then looked back at Jake.

"Jacob Knussli, these are better than Adel's."

"Better than mine?" Adel said.

"Well, aren't they?" Naomi asked her sister. "These are amazing. We need the recipe."

"I know how he made them."

"And from now on, we'll have to call them

Jacob's Superior Mashed Potatoes," Naomi said, and she burst out laughing when Adel swatted her arm.

"Superior, my foot!" Adel laughed. "Okay, they're very, very good. I will concede that they are equally as good as my own."

Jake chuckled. "I'll take it. I'm hungry, by the way."

"I'll check the chicken," Adel said, and headed toward the stove.

Naomi came over to where Jake stood and eyed him with a little smile on her face. "So you've spent your precious afternoon cooking with my sister instead of getting to know an available woman?"

"I did meet an available woman," he said, feeling just a little defensive. "Lydia is very nice."

"Is it set? Will you marry her?"

"No—" He shrugged. "I don't think she's quite right for me. Or me for her."

"Hmm." She nodded slowly. "You have what, two weeks to arrange this? No sense of urgency here?"

"Naomi, you're as bad as your sister. You two could be a matchmaking sister duo."

"We could be, because I see what my sister can't," Naomi said with a meaningful smile.

"I still think your perfect match is right under your nose. And she seems very pleased with your cooking. That's a rare quality around here."

He looked up to see Adel pulling the roasted chicken from the oven. Her face was pink from the heat of the stove, and when she closed the oven door, she pulled off the oven mitts and fanned herself with one of them.

The thought of cooking with Adel, talking with Adel…just spending time with her, was all very pleasant.

"Your sister doesn't want a husband," he said. "Besides, trying to convince my matchmaker to match with me would get me a very bad reputation around here. I'd never get a wife that way."

Naomi shrugged. "Suit yourself, Jake."

But Naomi's smile looked a little too smug for his liking. Maybe she had a point, though, and he was spending just a little too much time with his matchmaker instead of finding that match which would give him the farm.

Chapter Seven

That evening, Jake went to his uncle's farm to do the chores. The house was still locked up, covered in a yellow plastic tent, and it would be another two days before it was opened and he could go inside again. He'd be permanently locked out of this place if he didn't find a wife, though, and standing in front of the barn, looking out across the farmyard, he felt the depth of everything he would lose.

Gott, is it Your will that I get this farm in my name? he prayed silently. *Or do You have other plans for me? Should I be trying to let go of this farm instead of struggling to keep it?*

He wished at times like this that *Gott* would just give him a clear answer, but all he got in response was the chattering call of a blue jay in a nearby tree.

The cattle were out grazing in a far field, and Jake had tagged the ear of two new calves. The herd was growing. Since he'd come back, ten new calves had been born. But this wasn't just about bringing a rundown farm back from the brink. Jake had grown, too.

Living English, he'd forgotten the feeling of tired muscles mingled with the awe of watching a sunset over the fields. He'd forgotten the panic of a calf born limp and lifeless, and then watching it lift its head for the first time and feeling like that one weak bawl from a newborn held all the hope in the entire world. He'd matured into a man out there with the English, but he was deepening into the man he was born to be back home with the Amish.

Who would he be if he lost the family farm now? And would he have to find out?

He didn't know why he was feeling so fatalistic after meeting one woman, but he'd been looking at the available women in Redemption ever since he returned, and the only woman to spark his interest was his matchmaker—the one with reasons to keep herself single. Up until this point, he'd assumed that he'd meet someone. He'd certainly prayed that he would, and he'd truly believed that *Gott* would put a woman in his path who would fill his heart and give him the ability to be married in time to keep the farm. So having to use a matchmaker with the deadline steadily approaching was starting to feel desperate.

Jake headed back in the direction of the chicken coop. His shoulders were sore, but it did feel good to be out in the open air, working a job where he could see the results and feel the good he was doing on a heart-deep level. If nothing else, he was learning where he belonged, and it wasn't back with the English.

"Jacob!"

He shaded his eyes to see his neighbor, Corny Moser, at the fence. Corny was a man nearing fifty with a houseful of *kinner* and a plump, serious wife.

"How are you?" Jake called as he headed in the man's direction.

"Good, good." Corny leaned against the rail. "How's the fumigation going?"

"Two more days, and then they'll let me back inside," he said.

"Yah, yah..." Corny chewed the side of his cheek. "I heard some rumors about your inheritance being in question?"

"It's not final unless I'm married," Jake replied.

Corny pulled off his hat and inspected it. "*Yah*, I heard that. I have a younger sister coming to visit me next month. She's thirty-five, has three *kinner* from her first marriage, and she's a good cook. She's also good with cattle—which is something you don't think of right off when looking for a wife, but it's real useful. There are times you need a woman to do more than open and close gates for you, you know? Like when the calving is going strong, or when you're getting ready for market. So a woman who can pitch in is real helpful when you're starting out and don't have a pile of nephews or cousins to pitch in, you know?"

Corny looked up then and met Jake's gaze seriously.

"That's something to think about," Jake replied.

"*Yah*. It's something to consider. I didn't think about it when I married Ruth, but it turns out she's good with cattle. They like her. She's got the touch, you know? She can stand at the fence and sing and she'll get a whole audience of cattle who come to just listen."

"I didn't know that," Jake said, and he thought fondly back to his own *mamm*'s singing—not quite the kind that would call up cattle from the field, though.

"I can introduce you when she comes," Corny said. "You could come for dinner at our place, and maybe take her for a stroll."

"Honestly, Corny, I need a wife in a week and a half," he replied.

"That soon?" Corny shot him a look of surprise. "Why'd you put it off so long?"

"I didn't!" Jake insisted. "I was looking, talking to available women, saying hello…"

"Not saying you wanted a wife," Corny replied. "That's a different message altogether."

"Maybe so, but I was hoping for love," Jake replied.

"Right. Right." He nodded a couple of times.

"How did you meet Ruth?" Jake asked.

"She was in the youth group. I asked her home from singing."

Jake's youth group days were behind him, nor did he want a wife half his age. But he could see how he'd missed out on that prime time for pairing off when young couples took the plunge. It was how Alphie had met his wife, too. It wasn't quite so easy at his age.

"But you fell in love with her, right?" Jake asked.

"*Yah.* That's how it works in a buggy in the

moonlight," Corny said with a chuckle. "You should try it. And if you're still single when my sister gets here, we'll have that dinner."

"If I'm still single when your sister gets here, I won't have a farm," he replied seriously.

Corny pressed his lips together and didn't answer that. Perhaps he was rethinking his offer of introduction. Because without a farm, what could Jake actually offer a woman? Just his heart? At eighteen, a girl would accept that from a boy she loved. Now? He'd better have more.

"Do you have a backup plan?" Corny asked after some silence.

"I have some money tucked away, and I would find some work of some sort—farm-work, hopefully," he replied.

"You should have come home sooner," Corny said. "Coming back now is like starting from scratch where a twenty-year-old kid starts."

"I know it." Jake clenched his teeth together, trying to push back his own rising frustration.

"That's like fifteen years lost..." Corny seemed to be talking more to himself. "Fifteen years of building a career around here, a reputation. *Englisher* work is different."

"I know, I know," Jake said. There was no turning back time. "But if I get married in time, I've got the family land back, and when I have *kinner*, I'll have something to leave them."

Corny nodded. "That would be best. I sympathize, Jacob. I really do."

Corny Moser hadn't wasted his time, and neither had most of the community. Starting life was important to the Amish, and Jake had missed out.

"I need to finish up chores tonight," Jake said. "If you're so inclined, send up a prayer for me that I'll find the right woman in time."

"I'll certainly do that," Corny replied. "Remember what I said about buggies in the moonlight. I'm a firm believer that they aid the process very nicely."

Jake chuckled. "Thanks. I'll keep it in mind."

Jake tapped the fence in farewell and he headed back in the direction of the chicken coop. Corny's sister wouldn't arrive soon enough for Jake to inherit this land, and wherever he looked, he was faced with memories. Corny was right, though, he'd come home too late. If he'd returned sooner, his uncle might have put him in the will without this silly requirement that he be married.

Alphie was married now. He'd found a wife, and they had three little ones. Alphie had the Amish life that Jake had missed out on. And Alphie had been so full of gossip to pass along, the stories that kept Jake from coming home.

Jake couldn't really blame anyone but himself, but he had a few residual feelings left for Alphie, too. He'd visited him a few times since his return, and looking around Alphie's Amish sitting room, with a plump wife in the kitchen and little ones playing overhead, he'd felt a wash of jealousy. That and his growing sense that perhaps he'd listened too much to his cousin's family tales that kept him away from Alphie now.

He had no one to blame but himself, but he'd also trusted the wrong source of information about what was happening at home. Not everyone's interest in his life was selfless. Some people saw entertainment in someone else's difficulty—not intentionally, but it was what it boiled down to—and Jake was the one who had to live with the fallout.

The sun had just set, leaving a crimson glow along the horizon. Adel sat on the porch with a kerosene lamp to illumine her knitting.

She was making a scarf. In the later months of the year, the tourists who visited their bed-and-breakfast liked having some handmade items to purchase, and Adel was working on her stash of them that would be for sale.

She heard the plod of hooves as Jake sent his horse into the pasture, and then the click of the gate locking shut again. Sounds seemed to carry farther in the night air with nothing to compete with but the hum of insects and the creak of her porch swing as she gently rocked back and forth.

She put her knitting aside for a moment, and inspected a burn on her wrist. She'd gotten it when cleaning the coals out of the oven that evening. They hadn't been as cool as she'd thought. She picked up her knitting again; the familiar looping of yarn and clicking of needles was soothing. She didn't have to think when she knitted—her hands knew the work.

"Are you waiting up for me?" Jake's deep voice broke through the stillness, and she looked over her shoulder to see him coming up to the house.

"Sort of," she replied. "I like to sit out here and think. It's soothing."

"Where's your sister?" he asked.

"She's in bed."

"You want company?" he asked.

She should say no. She should send him in and use the opportunity to smooth down her own feelings, but when she found his gentle gaze locked on her face, she didn't have the heart to turn him away.

She lifted the skein of yarn. "You can hold my wool, if you like. Don't tell me you knit, too."

Jake laughed, and he took a seat on the swing next to her, dutifully holding the skein of yarn in one palm. "No, I don't knit. You're safe from having to explain *that*."

His arm was warm against hers, and he smelled faintly of hay and sunshine. He took over rocking the swing, his long legs pushing them farther than she'd been able to, and she enjoyed the sensation of just letting go.

"So what are you thinking about out here?" he asked.

"You." She felt her face heat, and she dropped a stitch. "I mean…getting you a match."

"Of course." He slowed the rocking while she picked free her mistake and got it back on the needle. "What are my chances here?"

"I don't know," she admitted. "It's in *Gott*'s

hands, as is every marriage. I'm going to do my best to find you a good and virtuous woman. The decision you two make will be up to you."

"My neighbor suggested I meet his sister," he said. "She's a little older than me, has three *kinner*. But she won't be in Redemption in time, and when he realized that it would be past the date for getting the farm in the mix, I think he cooled to the idea."

"Hmm." She continued knitting. "He wanted two family farms right next to each other. It's understandable."

"Yah," he said quietly. "But it made me think… Who am I without a farm, Adel?"

She glanced up at him. "You're Jacob Knussli."

"Yah, but what do I have to offer if I have no paid-off farm?" he said. "I realized that I've wasted fifteen years."

"You have yourself, Jake," she said. "And that's the difference between a marriage of convenience and a marriage for love. If you marry for love, you're both willing to sacrifice a lot to be together."

"The farm won't matter?" he asked.

"For the right woman."

"Will I find that kind of love, though?"

Adel put down her knitting. "I'm going to

tell you a story that Mark told over and over again to young people looking for love."

"All right."

"When you want a barn, you don't look around yourself for one that has simply dropped from the sky ready-made, do you?"

Jake chuckled. "No."

"That's right. You look for the spot. You look for a piece of farmland close to the house, but far enough away to give you some space to live. You need a place that is a little higher so it won't flood during storms. You need a spot that is level and that is just the right distance from the fields. And then, you build it."

Jake was silent, and her mind went back to when her husband would tell that story to some young man thinking about marriage.

"I hated that story," she said softly.

"What?"

"I did," she confessed. "It's very wise, but what he was saying was that you find a woman who has good characteristics, and then you build a life with her. It's what he did with me."

"That's not a good thing?" he asked.

"It is a good thing. It's the very advice I'm giving you," she replied. "But for me... It sounded like he hadn't really loved me, but he'd learned to. Or he knew he could, if he just tried. I was young and I didn't like to hear that I was just a good collection of characteristics he could learn to love."

She was probably saying too much, but there was something about a cool evening, the velvet darkness and the warm pool of kerosene light around them that softened the moment.

"I'm sure you were much more than that," Jake said, and his voice was firm. "I'm serious, Adel. From what you've told me about him, he respected you deeply. He went to you for your insight into situations. He loved you."

"He did love me." She knew it. "But that story rankled me all the same."

Jake smiled faintly. "I'm glad you told me that."

"Does it help?" she asked.

He shook his head. "It means you trust me. You haven't told anyone else that, have you?"

Adel dropped her gaze. He'd guessed right. "No, I haven't."

"A wife is more than a collection of good character traits," he said quietly. "She's not just a woman in the kitchen, or a woman hanging your laundry. She's the one you come home to, both physically and emotionally. She's the one who will build you up when you feel weak, make you feel like you can face life's challenges again. She's the one who will brighten your home and make it sunny during rainy days. And she's the one you work every backbreaking hour to provide for, because you want her to have everything she could ever need. And I think if a man is really blessed, that wife will open up to him and show him the tender parts inside of her, too."

Adel's breath caught. It was beautiful... His gaze dropped down to her wrist and he frowned.

"What happened?" He caught her hand in his and turned it over to expose the burn on the inside of her wrist.

"I was cleaning the stove," she whispered.

"Ouch," he said in sympathy, and he ran his thumb over the tender flesh beside the burn. He didn't let go of her hand, either, as if he'd forgotten he was holding it, and while she knew she should pull back, the moment to do so gracefully had passed.

"I don't want to tell a woman that she simply had potential, and so I married her," he said quietly. "I want to be able to tell her that I fell in love with her. If I'm to build a life, choose a spot and start nailing together a life with a woman, then what better foundation than love?"

"Do you have time for that?" she breathed.

He ran his fingers in a tingling line down her palm, and then released her hand.

"If I'm building a life, and the foundation is a piece of land and a woman who'd like the financial security of living there, I'm not sure that I'll feel secure. Not on a heart level. And yet, I have to offer a woman something more than this battered heart of mine."

"You want to be loved," she said softly, and the realization brought tears to her eyes. He'd been talking all this time about finding a woman he felt a spark with, but it went deeper than that. Jacob wanted a woman to love him back... It was the only thing that brought any kind of security in a relationship.

"Yah." He leaned back, his arm pressed against hers. "I'd very much like to be loved."

For a couple of minutes they swung gently together in silence, her knitting forgotten.

"For what it's worth," she said quietly, "I do think that a true and honest heart is the most important thing a man can offer."

But there was no time for him to fully explore that with any of the women she was introducing to him. Unless *Gott* moved and showed Jake beyond a shadow of a doubt that the woman he chose was *Gott*'s will for him.

"But the farm is what will draw them in," he said, his voice low. "A man's heart is important, but so is his ability to provide."

If only Jake had come to her a few months sooner, she might have had more time to help him find a love match. It was heartbreaking now to think of a man with such a longing for love settling for less. Because even though he was a rebel, and even though he was formed by his *Englisher* years spent away, Jacob Knussli deserved that.

Chapter Eight

~❧~

Dear Gott, Adel prayed while she lay in bed that night. *Guide Jacob to the woman You have for him. Show him Your will. Give him the love he longs for...*

A cool breeze came in the open bedroom window, ruffling the curtain and cooling her bare arms. She lay with the blanket and sheet flung back, too hot for covers.

And when You do provide that wife for him, help me to be happy for him—truly and sincerely. Help me to let go.

Because as much as she hated to admit it, Adel was getting attached to her very first client. She had started out more protective of the women in Redemption, not wanting them to be taken advantage of or have their hearts broken, but somehow her emotional investment had changed. Now, she was seeing Jake's sensitive heart, his deeper longings, and she was feeling more than she should be.

Perhaps this was a chance for her to grow, too. It was time for her to learn how to draw a line between herself and others, to keep her emotions in check. She no longer had a husband to help with that. When a woman was married, her heart belonged to her husband, and everyone understood when she took an emotional step back from the men in the community. It was right and good.

But she was no longer married. There was no husband to offend…there was no husband to turn her emotions toward. She had to learn how to be more selfless, and to work for the good of others without anything in return. And to keep her heart secure in the process.

And yet, she would get something in return—a position in this community, respect from the other men and women and the knowledge that her presence here in Redemption truly did make a difference. It was the kind of return that took time, and self-control, and maturity. She'd been praying for this exact thing in her life for the last few years, and *Gott* was giving it to her! But like anything, getting what she wanted felt differ-

ent from how she'd imagined it would, and
it would take more strength than she'd ever
dreamed.

Adel fell asleep that night, the sheet and
blanket flung back so that she could feel the
cool breeze on her feet and her arms, and
she had the sense that she was changing, too.
Growth was rarely comfortable—Mark said
that often. And *Gott* was giving her a chance
at the life she'd prayed for.

It was time for her to step up and accept
the challenge.

The next morning, Adel and Jake arrived at
the Swarey Flower Farm. Delia Swarey sold
flowers to local florists, as well as to vendors
looking for blooms for weddings and the like.
She had massive gardens that she and her four
sons tended, as well as greenhouses that extended her growing season well into the fall
with a few specialized plants that she tended
through the winter, as well.

As Jake unhitched the horse, Adel sank
into a chair in Delia's kitchen.

"Jake is younger than me," Delia said.

"By two years," Adel said. "That's not such
a big deal this side of thirty, is it?"

"Not as much," Delia agreed. "It's the maturity that matters. You think he's…mature enough for this family?"

Adel nodded. "I wouldn't have brought him here if I didn't think so. I've seen a side to him that he keeps hidden from most people, and he's a wonderful man. He's kind, considerate, a deep thinker. And he's glad to be home in the Amish world again."

"Did he come for the inheritance?" Delia asked. "That's something that worries me. You said that he only gets the farm if he's married. I don't need a farm. I have the flower farm here, and I'm managing all right. This wouldn't be about money for me."

"I wouldn't be so crass as to suggest it," Adel said earnestly. "It isn't about money for him, either."

"How do you know?" Delia asked. "He would say that, wouldn't he?"

She knew because she'd spent some time with him, listening to him, reading his expressions when he shared his deeper feelings. Jake was a special man, and while he came across as charming and handsome without much else to him, that couldn't be further from the truth. Yet, how could she explain that to Delia?

"At first I worried about that, too," Adel said. "Coming home to Redemption was a complicated experience for him. His uncle Johannes wasn't exactly welcoming, so it wouldn't have been an easy return, especially after his *daet*'s death. But Jacob is back now because he truly wants to be here."

"What did he say?" Delia pressed. "What convinced you?"

But those conversations felt precious, somehow, and she'd assured him that she could be discreet.

"You'll have to ask him about it, and see what I mean," Adel said.

Jake had deepened more than anyone might realize, and she'd seen such a tender core to him that it made her feel a strange urge to protect him, to encourage him. It gave her a glimpse into the depth of emotional intimacy he had to offer a woman he trusted with his heart.

"Are you ready to get married again?" Adel asked softly.

"I miss Zeke a lot," Delia said. "You understand, I know, because you lost Mark."

"I do." Adel nodded. "It's hard."

"Very hard." Delia sucked in a deep breath. "But my boys are running wild on me, and I could use some help in raising them. Jacob isn't a *daet*, though. He might not understand how I love my boys."

"There also isn't the complication of blending a family of stepsiblings," Adel pointed out.

Delia nodded. "Good point. What does he think of me?"

"He's here, isn't he?" Adel asked. "He's a bit overwhelmed with this process of finding a wife this quickly."

She felt a little twinge at sharing that personal detail about Jake. Did he want her to tell that to his prospective matches? Or was Adel just feeling protective of her deeper discussions with Jake? Delia was a good woman, and she had a big heart. Of anyone, Adel was sure she could love her second husband dearly, and Jake needed that.

"I talked to my boys this morning about the possibility of me getting married again, and them having a new *daet*," Delia said.

"What did they think?" Adel asked.

"They thought it was too soon," she said. "They miss their *daet* a lot. They did everything with him. They talk about the things he said, and the way he did things all the time. When I told them that you wanted to introduce me to a man looking for a wife, they said they wanted to meet him before I do." Delia shrugged and laughed softly. "They're such protective boys."

Adel looked out the window. Jake was standing with Delia's oldest son, Ezekiel.

"They look like they're getting along," Adel said.

Delia leaned forward to look, too. "*Yah*, they do…"

"They don't want a new father in their lives?" Adel asked.

"I don't think they know what they want," Delia said. "They miss Zeke, but he's not coming back. And we do need a man around here to give them an example. They can't only work with a memory."

"They want to take care of you themselves?" Adel asked.

"They do." Delia nudged a plate of pastries closer to Adel. "But that won't work when they have sweethearts of their own, will it? Of course, they're boys, and they don't see that." She sighed. "I miss having someone to lean on."

"I think you're doing a great job with them," Adel said. "But I know what you mean about missing that support."

Adel missed it, too. There was something about the strength of a husband that no other relationship could replace.

"I wouldn't say this to anyone else, but I

know you understand, Adel," Delia said, lowering her voice. "I miss being kissed. Zeke used to kiss my forehead on his way past, and it was just such a little thing, but I miss that. I miss being hugged—not by a son, but by a man I'll go to sleep with, and wake up next to."

Adel swallowed. Yes, she missed all of that, too.

"I feel guilty for missing it so much," Delia said.

"Don't," Adel said. "It's normal. And I do believe that *Gott* gives us that longing for connection for a reason. He places the lonely in families, remember? There is nothing wrong with yearning for the very thing that *Gott* provides!"

"But you've gone much longer on your own," Delia said. "And you seem fine."

"*Gott* has different paths for all of us," Adel said. And she'd truly believed these last five years that *Gott* was not leading her toward another marriage. But now, at the least opportune time, she was yearning for all those things that Delia yearned for. Adel wasn't as "fine" as she seemed.

Adel looked out the window again, and this time she saw that the other three boys had materialized from somewhere. The boys were standing around, one digging his boot into the gravel, another with his thumbs stuck in his suspenders. Ezekiel's arms were crossed over his chest and he straightened up to his full height, just a few inches shorter than Jake was. Delia had promised her boys that they could talk to Jake first, and Adel couldn't help but wonder what tests they were putting him through.

Jake looked toward the house, and he met Adel's gaze with a look of perplexed panic. She couldn't help but chuckle.

"I wonder what the boys are saying," Adel said.

"I wonder..." Delia murmured.

Jake could see Adel in the window, and Delia standing behind her. But it was Adel's serious, clear gaze that met his. What he wouldn't give for Adel at his side right now, because the four teenagers weren't responding to any of his attempts to be friendly.

"How come you lived English?" the oldest, Ezekiel, asked. "You were English for a really long time, too. We know an older boy who went English during his *Rumspringa*, but only for a few months. He was back before spring."

"I'm glad he came back so quickly," Jake said. "That was wise of him."

"Why didn't you?" Thomas pressed. He was younger than Ezekiel, but stood an inch taller, just about as tall as Jake was. "You're avoiding the question."

"You're speaking to your elder," Jake said.

"I'm only asking what my mother will ask you," Ezekiel replied. "She said we could ask you the questions that mattered most to us. And this one matters."

"There were other pressures," Jake said. "My father and I didn't get along, and when he passed away, I didn't think my uncle would be glad to see me."

"We lost our father," Thomas said. "And nothing would chase us away from our responsibilities right here at home."

"Are you old enough for your *Rumspringa*?" Jake asked.

"He's not, but I'm old enough." Ezekiel met his gaze like an equal. "I'm skipping mine. I don't need to go wild to find out what's important."

"I'm glad to hear you have the maturity," Jake said. "Your *mamm* raised you well."

"My *daet* raised us all well." There was some defiance in that gaze.

"We heard you've got a farm," one of the younger boys said. This was Aaron, and he looked to be about fifteen.

"*Yah.* I *will* have a farm…" How much was he supposed to say to teenagers? This was a conversation that should be happening between adults. He looked toward the house again. The women weren't in the window. The boys had been permitted to question him, and they were perceptive, and not inclined to trust him, it seemed. Should he just walk away from them? This was where he needed Adel's advice.

"You'll only have the farm if you marry our *mamm*." That was from the youngest boy—Moses. "We know that."

"You want our *mamm* to marry you for the inheritance," Ezekiel said. "She'd be useful to you."

That sparked anger, and Jake sent the boy an annoyed look.

"Women are not tools to be used. I haven't even discussed this with your mother," Jake said. "And I won't discuss it with the four of you."

"Our *mamm* said you *have* to talk to us

first," Moses said, squaring his not-quite-grown shoulders. "We're the men here."

Jake sighed. "You're boys."

"She didn't exactly say that," Thomas said to his brother.

"But she won't marry him if we tell her we won't accept him," Aaron retorted.

Jake rubbed a hand over his eyes.

"What do you want in a wife?" Ezekiel asked.

Jake shut his eyes for a moment, praying for patience. "I want a good woman who loves *Gott*."

"That's very broad," Ezekiel said dryly. "That's all that matters to you? So she'll be the one who cooks your meal, cleans your home…and that's all that matters to you? What about her happiness? I doubt picking up after you is all that fun. We want our *mamm* to be happy."

Ezekiel was old enough now at seventeen to have a few opinions of his own, and if Jake were on the outside of this, he'd be impressed with the boy's strength of resolve.

"All right. You want to talk like men?" Jake's patience was spent. "I want more than just a good woman. You're right. Marriage isn't just about a man who works outdoors and a woman who takes care of the house. There's a whole lot more to a happy home than shared work. And that is why discussing the finer details with the four of you doesn't help anything." Jake looked at the glowering faces before him. "You don't like me, do you?"

"Not a lot," Moses said. Jake smiled grimly at the youngest boy, and he shuffled uncomfortably, stepping back.

"Don't let him intimidate you," Ezekiel said to his brother, then turned back to Jake. "If we don't like you, how do you expect to be our *daet*?"

"It wouldn't be easy," Jake said soberly. "This would have to work for the whole family, and it's not just about the adults."

"You better believe that," Aaron muttered.

"So with the understanding that you all can't stand me," Jake said with a small smile, "will you at least let me talk with your mother? If you have as much sway as you say, then I don't have a hope, anyway. But I can't even leave until your mother and I have spoken. They're waiting for me in there."

The boys exchanged a look among them. They could obviously see the reasoning there. They were the *kinner* in this home, after all, and their mother was the final say.

"*Yah*, all right," Ezekiel said.

Jake eyed them for a moment, but they stared back at him in silence. There was nothing reassuring he could say to them. He was here to discuss the possibility of marriage with their mother, and they'd rather see the back of him. So he sighed and headed toward the house without another word.

Jake tapped on the door and opened it. They were expecting him, after all. He found the women in the kitchen. He caught Adel's eye first, wondering what the tone was in here. If the boys were that antagonistic toward him, was Delia going to even want to entertain this? Should they just leave now?

"Jacob Knussli, you remember Delia Swarey," Adel said. "We saw you chatting with the boys."

"*Yah.*" He smiled faintly. "They...are a protective bunch."

"Oh, they are that," Delia said with a fond smile. "They figured that you should talk to them first, man to man. I didn't see the harm. They're sweet boys."

Downright adorable, he thought wryly.

"Have a seat?" Adel prompted.

"Yes, do sit down," Delia said. "Would you like a pastry?"

Delia had a nice smile, and an easy way about her. She was older than Lydia, and she had some lines around her eyes, but she still looked youthful enough. But he could feel the same thing he'd felt with Lydia already. They were both perfectly nice women with so much to offer…and just not for him.

"Thank you," he said, accepting an apple pastry, flaky and delicate. "This looks delicious…"

"Delia makes the best apple strudel," Adel said. "I've bought some of her strudel to serve at the bed-and-breakfast. No one can bake it flakier here in Redemption. That's a guarantee."

Jake took a bite—he had to taste it now—and he chewed slowly. Adel was right. He'd never eaten a better strudel. Now they'd make small talk about strudel and gardening, or whatever it was they decided to talk about that wasn't the real reason why he was here. Because when they did discuss what they wanted in life, it wouldn't be so terribly different. They'd both want an Amish home with peace and happiness inside those walls. But the boys needed someone they could respect and accept, and that wasn't going to happen in a matter of days.

Those boys loved their *mamm*, and they wanted to keep her safe. If he did manage to win them over, it would happen with persistence and time—the one luxury he didn't have. And plowing forward to marry their *mamm* would ruin any attempts at a relationship with them in the future. This wasn't about marrying a woman. For the Swarey home, it was about building a family. That was too precious to rush.

Finding a wife wasn't turning out to be a very simple thing. The Bible said, "House and riches are the inheritance of fathers: and a prudent wife is from the Lord." The more he thought about it, the truer those words rang. A wife was a gift from above.

Gott, *guide me,* he prayed.

An hour later, Jake sat in the buggy, fiddling with the reins. Adel was still in the house—she'd stayed to talk to Delia alone with him safely out of earshot. The boys, who'd helped him hitch his horse back up in record time, had retreated to the stable, but when Jake leaned over to look in their direction, he found all four of them eyeing his buggy uncomfortably, and when they saw that he'd spotted them, they sauntered off toward the house with exaggerated nonchalance.

He turned forward again. The side door opened and Adel came out of the house. The boys headed up the steps, looking over their shoulders in his direction.

"Ezekiel, you've grown again," Adel said with a smile. "And Moses, Thomas, Aaron—every time I see you you're bigger! What does your mother feed you?"

The boys all seemed to soften toward Adel, and shy smiles broke over their faces. They murmured replies, and Adel turned and said something to Delia, who stood in the doorway. Delia gave him a friendly look, but nothing more.

When Adel pulled herself up into the buggy, the door closed firmly behind the boys, and the horse started forward. Jake licked his lips and glanced down at Adel.

"They are really nice boys," Adel said.

Jake gave her a wry look. "Are they?"

"*Yah.* Very good *kinner.* They work hard for their *mamm.* That flower farm flourishes because of their hard work."

He nodded. "They don't like me much."

"Their *daet* only died two years ago, and I really did think they'd be more ready to accept a new *daet*," Adel said, casting him an apologetic look. "I had a good talk with Delia, and she said that she can't rush anything without her boys' cooperation."

"That's understandable," he said.

"She likes you," Adel said. "She said she thinks you'll make someone a very good husband, but unfortunately, she can't look any further into a marriage."

"She's a very nice person, too," he said, and he felt an unexpected wave of relief.

"I'm really sorry," Adel said. "It's my fault. I really thought she'd be more eager to get a man back into her home, but... I didn't think far enough ahead. And I should have."

"Hey, it's fine—" He reached out instinctively and squeezed her hand. He hadn't thought before he did it, but her soft fingers felt good in his. She was a comfort.

"You have so much to offer a wife," Adel said. "I know this is rushed, but I truly do believe you have so much to give. I just need to be able to show people what I see, and I feel like I failed there with Delia."

He looked over at her. Her hand was still in his, and she looked so full of remorse, he could have hugged her right there. Instead, he let go of her hand.

"You didn't fail," he said. "It wasn't the right match. That's all."

Jake reined the horse in where the drive met the road.

Adel thought he had a lot to offer… Somehow that warmed him in a way nothing else could. She saw the man in him, and even if it was entirely unhelpful right now, he saw the woman in her.

"Do you have to get back?" he asked, glancing over at her.

"Not really," she replied. "Why?"

"Because I want ice cream." He flicked the reins and guided the horse onto the paved road. "Some days, after being particularly humbled, a man just needs some caramel ripple."

Chapter Nine

Somehow, Adel had been preparing herself to let Delia down, not the other way around. And she wasn't sure why Jake being rejected by a potential match had pricked her heart quite this way, but it had. At first, she might have thought that a rejection would bother him, but she had misjudged Jake, too. She'd discovered a softer center to the man than she ever guessed existed. Not only did he have good intentions in what he wanted to offer a wife, but Jacob wanted to be loved, too.

And yet, there was this one, selfish, wicked part of her that was happy that Delia had pulled back—not because she wanted to see Jake hurt, but because it meant she had a little more time getting to know this complicated man. It was an unlikely friendship, but one that was sinking under all her defenses.

"Ice cream does improve a day," Adel said.

"*Yah*. It does." He flicked the reins, and her gaze was drawn to his strong, broad hands.

"Have you been going to the Aberdeen Dairy often?" she asked, recognizing the route.

"No." He glanced down at her, and a playful smile tickled the corner of his lips. "But I've driven by the place often enough, and I kept telling myself I'd stop in when I had more time."

"At least you're taking the time now," she said. "That's a very *Englisher* way of looking at things—not having time."

"Maybe." He smiled faintly, and he fell silent. His expression turned cloudy and he kept his gaze locked on the road.

"I didn't mean to offend," she said after a moment.

"What?" He looked over at her. "It's not you. Sorry. Not you at all. It's something I had on my mind last night and can't get rid of. I've been thinking that it's probably time I hashed a few things out with my cousin, but I wanted to wait until I knew whether the farm was mine or not before I did."

"You said you've visited him," she said.

"*Yah*," he replied. "But I've never said my

piece. The thing is, I believed him. I listened to him and I took his perspective seriously. And he was so eager to gather up these stories that kept me distanced from my family and pass them along to me, so supportive of me not coming home…"

"Do you think he wanted the land?" she asked.

He shook his head slowly. "No. He was plenty surprised when he found out he'd get it if I didn't get married. And he didn't think he had any hope of that farm coming to him because he was convinced I'd find a wife. I believe him about that. No, he passed along stories to me because he enjoyed telling them. And he passed stories back to my father and uncle for the same reason. He liked being involved. He liked being the bearer of news."

"A gossip," she murmured.

"Is that what it is?" He sighed, then shook his head. "He was married, had *kinner*, and he was so supportive of me living my life on my own terms. He would never judge, he said. Well, I wish he'd judged a little bit. Because me staying away benefited him more than any of us anticipated."

"Have you told the bishop about this?" Adel asked.

He shook his head. "And I won't. It's my personal business. I'll talk to my cousin myself. I don't need church leadership involved. This is a family issue."

The short, brightly painted ice cream shop was ahead with a sign that read Aberdeen Dairy. It was set back from the road a little way, nestled next to a treed area, and beyond it was the actual dairy farm. It was modern and spread out, bright new buildings shining in the sunlight with a generous parking lot that made use of the shade from the trees. Some families occupied a few picnic tables in amid the trees, as well. One *Englisher* couple sat on the lowered tailgate of a big red pickup truck as they ate ice cream sundaes, and they looked up in idle curiosity as Adel and Jake parked the buggy next to a horse rail. This was an *Englisher*-owned-and-operated shop that many Amish people frequented, but this morning, there were mostly cars and pickup trucks in the parking lot.

Jake held the door for Adel, and they went into the comforting blast of air-conditioning. Adel shivered in pleasure and scanned the menu board.

"Whatever you want," Jake said. "It's my treat."

Adel went over to look into the freezer where the buckets of ice cream sat, rows of creamy, colorful swirls. There were a few people ahead of them in line, so there was time. Jake stood next to her for a moment, his arm just a whisper from hers, and she could feel the warmth of him next to her.

"You deserve some payoff for all the work you're putting in with me," he said.

"It's not all misery," she said jokingly.

"Good." She glanced up and he was closer to her than she'd thought he'd be, and his gaze dragged over her face, then he took a step back. "I'm just going to check the corkboard for job listings."

Adel surveyed her favorite ice cream choices—peach, raspberry, mint chocolate chip... When she looked up again, she saw Jake tearing a phone number off a posting.

"Next!" the cashier called, and Jake came over to join her at the counter.

"Hi," Jake said. "Can we get two large cones, please? One caramel ripple and one—" He looked at her.

"Peach, please."

Generous scoops of ice cream were loaded into sugar cones, and Jake pulled out his wallet to pay. Then they headed back to a free booth. Adel took a lick of ice cream as she sat down, but her gaze was on that little slip of paper he ripped from the board.

"You have a farm," she said quietly.

Jake laid the piece of paper on the tabletop next to his napkin. "Alphie might very well have that farm. I'm trying to be prepared."

"But what about faith?"

"I'm praying, Adel," he said quietly. "I pray constantly. But *Gott* doesn't always give us exactly what we pray for. He gives us what is good for us—and we don't always see the bigger picture."

"There is the kind of faith that accepts what *Gott* gives and chooses not to question," she said quietly. "And then there is the kind of faith, like the children of Israel at the Jordan River. Nothing happened until their toes touched the water."

"I think I'm already fully invested," he said. "If that's what you mean."

"Are you?" She looked down at the slip of paper with telephone number and address. "I think we need to put our feet into the Jordan, Jake. This isn't done yet. You're still meeting prospective matches."

He sighed. "I'm doing my best, Adel."

He was—she could see that. But Adel hadn't given up yet.

"When is your house open again after fumigation?" she asked.

"Today, actually. I swept it out this morning after I did chores. The opened it up for me a day early."

"Excellent timing." She took another bite of ice cream. "Let's get to work on your kitchen. You want to be prepared in case everything falls apart around you. But I think you should be prepared for *Gott* to answer your prayer and give you a wife."

He smiled faintly. "What are my chances here, Adel?"

"With just me and our best intentions?" she said. "That's anyone's guess. But with *Gott* working? Your chances suddenly turn into certainties. Have some faith, Jake."

His gaze softened. "I'm a little bit embarrassed to have you see it."

"I won't judge your home," she said softly. "I've already gotten to know you again, and I know how hard you've worked. But let's get it straightened up so there is less to explain to a wife."

"You're a treasure, Adel," he said quietly.

The word was the same one Mark used

to use, and her breath caught. A treasure…
And something inside her yearned to hear it
again from his mouth. To be truly treasured
by a man was a unique and wonderful experience…

She had to stop this. She was helping find
a wife. She wasn't the one he'd treasure going
forward. She was here for the transition, and
then she'd have to step back.

It was best not to forget that when his voice
was low and his warm gaze locked on hers.
Because Jacob Knussli was turning out to be
very, very easy to fall for.

When they arrived at the farm, Jake reined
in the horse and eyed the farmhouse warily.
That old house, the place that held so many
memories, was also one he was ashamed of.
He'd worked much harder on the farm than
he had on the house, and he wasn't even sure
why.

"I can start on the kitchen while you do
chores," Adel said.

"You could, but—" He swallowed. "I
mean, if you felt like coming with me to do
the chores, we could—"

"Jake, putting this off won't make it any
easier," she said. "I've seen many kitchens

before. I've helped families clean out a dead relative's house before, too. I've helped clean out bedrooms from the bedridden. I understand how big a mess can get. There is no shame in needing help."

Did she know how big the emotional mess was for him, too? Because that was probably the bigger problem right now.

"Jake, you go do the work you need to do," she said. "And trust that I'll hold all judgment."

Trust her... He didn't have much choice, did he?

Jake unlocked the door and pushed it open. The kitchen was dim, the curtains all pulled shut, and there was the musty smell of old house to greet them. He scanned the familiar kitchen. He had one side of the table he kept clean for eating, but the rest of it was covered in junk from piles of old *Budget* newspapers to bottles of boot black, an old roasting pan, some baskets in a wobbling pile, two old spools from bailing twine. He should have thrown all of it away—just filled a wagon and made a trip to the dump—but it seemed like every day he dedicated to cleaning out this house left him facing a whole new mess underneath the last one.

"It's better than it was," he said, his face heating with embarrassment. "I had to throw out all sorts of rotting food when I got here. And I just emptied everything into the garbage. The rest is just clutter. My uncle didn't throw anything away. Believe it or not, I've actually cleared out a lot, but I started upstairs."

He hadn't been able to face sleeping in the clutter, and he'd completely emptied his old bedroom. Then he'd moved on to his late uncle's bedroom and hauled out a full wagonload of garbage. He'd burned it all one night, and watching it all go up in flames had been strangely therapeutic. He'd had the urge to do the same thing to the house—just burn it down to the foundation, but, of course, he wasn't crazy. The second floor was almost done now, but the downstairs had been more than he could tackle yet.

"It's okay." Adel picked up a dusty container of vinegar from the tabletop. "This is a great place to start. You'll see a big difference when you get back."

Jake turned to leave, then stopped. He marched back into the kitchen and flung back the curtains, letting rays of warm sunlight into the room. He went to the window over the sink and did the same thing. It was time to empty this old house of all the mustiness and garbage.

Then he shot Adel a wobbly smile. "I'll hurry up."

Jake put his back into his chores. He didn't want to leave Adel alone with that mess any longer than necessary. One of the reasons he hadn't asked for help was because he hadn't wanted to open that door to the women of the community. Then they'd see, and there was still a part of him that wanted to protect his family image, even though he'd run from it all himself.

When he finished the chores, his muscles ached and he was sweaty from work. He headed back toward the house just as the door opened and a rug was flung over the banister. Adel looked up and gave him a cheerful wave.

How could she be happy working on something like this? She'd maintained her own neat, organized home, and now to be faced with this mess? He noticed a pile of garbage she'd started off to the side.

"That can all be burned," Adel said when she noticed where his attention went.

"Okay," he said.

"Come and see how much I've gotten done

already," she said, leading the way inside. "I did peek upstairs—I hope you don't mind—and you did an incredible job up there, if down here is any indication of what you had to start with. So really, Jake, don't feel bad."

As he stepped into the kitchen, his heart skipped a beat. The kitchen table was completely clear, washed and even polished with some wood oil. The counters were covered in neat piles of dishes, and a cardboard box sat in the center of the room, where he could see some cracked and broken dishes inside. The whole room smelled of a mixture of mild bleach and vinegar.

"I'm cleaning every last surface," she said. "We have to get any residue off from the fumigation. It wouldn't be safe for you, otherwise."

"Yah." He smiled faintly. "Well, let me get scrubbing, too. What can I be working on?"

"Why don't you wipe out the cupboards while I wash all the dishes," she said.

Somehow, the mess seemed much more manageable with Adel by his side. He climbed a stepladder to reach better and accepted a rag that Adel handed to him. There was a bucket of soapy water sitting on the counter beneath him, and he got to work.

"I hope you don't mind, but I'm tossing anything that's broken," she said as she turned on the water at the sink.

"That makes sense," he said. A woman didn't want to be saddled with broken dishes. He looked down at Adel as she reached for a mismatched pile of bowls, and he spotted one on the top—ceramic with a red stripe around the side of it. It had a crack that started at a chip at the lip, and he suddenly froze.

Adel lifted the bowl, surveyed it for a moment and started in the direction of that cardboard box of discarded junk, and his heart nearly beat out of his chest.

"No!" he said suddenly.

Adel turned back. "What?"

"That bowl." He came down the ladder and took it from her hands. "It was my *mamm*'s favorite."

"Oh…" Adel nodded. "I'm sorry, I didn't know."

"How could you?" He felt his chin quiver. "Look, maybe this is a bad idea."

Adel was silent, and he looked around at the mess of a kitchen. It was coming together, and he knew that most of this was junk, but it was junk that was attached to his heart in the strangest of ways. He couldn't blame Alphie for keeping him away—he'd been running from more than Alphie ever realized.

"Jake?" Adel put a hand on his arm.

"I, uh—" He licked his lips. "Somehow burning this whole house down would be easier than going through it piece by piece."

"The bowl stays," she said softly. "We'll glue it. It'll last for years, if you're careful. The bowl stays."

Jake let out a slow breath. His mother had been the heart of this home, even when his grumpy uncle lived with them. She'd been the source of pleasant aromas, of comforting routine and of a list of rules as long as his arm. He missed those rules after her death, because no one told him to brush his teeth before coming downstairs, or to hang up his clothes neatly in the closet. No one made him eat vegetables, either, unless he felt like it. Or insisted upon pleases and thank-yous, or saying something nice even when he wanted to grumble. When *Mamm* died, they lost all the sunshine and civilization in the home. But a bowl wasn't going to bring her back.

"A wife isn't going to want some chipped, cracked bowl," he said. "Toss it."

"What?" Adel frowned.

"Throw it out. It's fine," he said, and he started to turn.

"No, it's not fine." She caught the front of his shirt to stop him. "Jake, these are your memories. This is your home."

"Is it? It won't be my kitchen once I'm married," he said. "I'm supposed to be getting ready for a wife, remember? This will be her domain, not mine."

"Any woman who wouldn't care about the bowl your late mother used when you were a boy isn't worthy of you!" Her voice shook, and she still didn't let go of him. "You don't have to sacrifice everything you care about for a wife."

"But that's not true, is it?" he said, his voice low and rough. "I'm hopefully getting married to *someone* in a week's time. I'm sacrificing a whole lot."

"The right woman—" she started.

"The truly right woman would be someone I spent time with," he said, and he ran a finger down her cheek. Her skin was soft, and she tipped her face toward his touch, and if it weren't for the bowl in her hands between them, he would do more. "She'd be someone who'd gotten to know me, gotten to understand me. She'd be someone I wanted to pull into my arms—"

She'd be someone a whole lot like Adel. She looked up at him, her lips parted, and the rest of his thought just seemed to seep away. Because he wanted a wife who made him feel like this.

Adel licked her lips and dropped her gaze. "I'm doing my best for you…"

"I'm not blaming you, Adel," he said. "This whole situation is stupid. My uncle didn't need to make this difficult, but he did. And I tried to do this the old-fashioned way and meet a woman, fall in love… It didn't work. But I'm starting to realize what I'm giving up for this farm. I've got a few ideals of my own, you know, and I have half a mind to just let Alphie take it."

Adel lifted her gaze to meet his. "Then keep this bowl—wherever you end up. Because even though you're upset right now, and this is a huge emotional tangle, you're going to be glad you did. I'm going to put it on the table where it's safe. But you keep it."

Jake gave her a weak smile. "You insist on taking care of me."

"Someone has to do it," she said softly. "And until there is…someone…to take over, I'm happy for it to be me."

It was the most selfless thing anyone had

done for him, and he felt a surge of tenderness toward her.

"Is it part of the job of being matchmaker?" he asked, a catch in his voice.

She shook her head. "No. It's part of being your friend."

He wished she hadn't said that, because the word *friend* put a fence between them, and right now he longed to be so much more to her than a friend.

"I appreciate it," he said. She met his gaze for a moment longer, then she turned and put the bowl in the center of the kitchen table.

"You'll see," she said. "We'll get this place cleaned up. And tomorrow there's a hymn sing and a game night going on at the Hochstetler farm. Who knows? Maybe with less pressure you'll see someone who interests you, and I can talk to her on your behalf."

Jake was looking at someone who interested him right now...and he realized in a rush that his growing feelings for Adel were a big part of his problem. He should think more clearly before he gave up this farm to his cousin.

Adel wasn't available, and he'd better figure out his life without her.

Chapter Ten

Late the next afternoon, Jake parked the buggy and unhitched the horse at Hannes Hochstetler's farm where a scattering of peach trees surrounded a generous garden. Hannes's daughter, Iris, and her new husband, Caleb, were living with Hannes for the first year of their marriage while Caleb saved for a place of their own, and the farm was thriving as a result.

A lot of the neighbors had come to the evening of fun, and Adel scanned the familiar faces. The teenagers had set up some volleyball on the lawn and were diving after the ball with shrieks of fun. Some young mothers had their babies on quilts, and they sat chatting together as the babies crawled, kicked and played. There was a group of older people already singing hymns together, several groups of men chatting and three long tables of food set out.

"Adel!" Adel's friend Bernice, a mother of three school-aged children, came up beside her and tweaked her arm. "I heard that you're acting as matchmaker these days."

"I am," Adel said with a smile.

"Any luck matching up Jacob Knussli?" she asked.

"Not yet," Adel replied.

"Why not match him with your sister?" Bernice asked. "She'd be perfect for him. And what a cook! I know you're glad to have her at the bed-and-breakfast, but Adel, she's just wasted there. She needs a family."

"My sister isn't interested," Adel replied. "I did try that already. And it isn't like I haven't tried to get her married, but I'm her sister, and what I think is good for her she thinks is boring."

"Sisters." Bernice chuckled. "I heard that Delia's boys weren't so keen on Jacob, either."

"That's already gotten around?" Adel winced.

"Well, Delia hasn't said a word, but her boys told my boys, and that's how word gets out. If there was more time, I think Delia would be a good match, too. She's been lonely since Zeke died."

"Yah," Adel said. "But *kinner* make it more complicated. Especially teens. I feel a little foolish even thinking that match would work now."

"It was worth the try," Bernice replied. "What about Sarai Peachy? She's twenty-five, single and very sweet."

"Maybe too young," Adel said quietly. "Only twenty-five. Twelve years younger than him."

"You were fifteen years younger than Mark," Bernice reminded her.

But Mark was different. Still, time was getting short for finding Jake a wife, and while Sarai was younger than Adel had hoped, she'd had a decent amount of time of being single to grow and mature...

"She's a sweet young woman," Bernice said. "And he does come with a paid-off farm. That's worth something. Or there's Verna Kauffman. She's about to head east to see if she can find someone marriageable out that way. We could save her the time."

Verna was closer to Jake's age, but she'd never been married. She was slim, a wonderful cook and full of energy. But somehow, she didn't strike Adel as the sort of woman who would interest Jake. Maybe she was wrong, though—it wouldn't be the first time.

Adel nodded. "She's a possibility, too. I'll introduce him around tonight. You never know what might stick."

But her heart sank just a little at the thought. Tonight, she might see Jake's eyes light up for another woman, and that would mean that she'd succeeded. Because he was handsome, kind and truly decent. If he found someone who interested him, barring some unruly teenagers to get in the way, Adel could open a woman's eyes to Jake's virtues.

Bernice looked in the direction of the buggies. "Well, he's coming back. I'll let you get to work. See you later, Adel."

As her friend left, Jake arrived at her side. He nudged her arm with his own and gave her a small smile.

"We're going to make the most of this evening," Adel said. "You are going to meet every available woman here who is at least twenty-five or older. So remember names of the women who interest you, and don't be shy about chatting with them. This is going to save us a great deal of time."

"You seem very confident," he said.

"Why wouldn't I be?" she asked. "You clean up nicely, Jacob Knussli."

He chuckled. "Thank you. I think."

"I have a couple of women to introduce you to," Adel said, shooting him a smile. "In fact, they're both over there playing lawn darts."

"With Naomi?"

"Yah." Naomi, Verna and Sarai were all playing the game together. Sarai looked particularly pretty this evening, and Adel heard the ripple of her laughter as she did a bad throw.

"Who is the one in pink?" he asked.

Yah. He'd already spotted her. Adel tried to put more enthusiasm in her voice. "That's Sarai Peachy. She's twenty-five now, and a very nice woman."

"Hmm." He looked down at Adel, and for a moment he just met her gaze. Then he sighed. "Should we get this over with?"

Was that for her benefit? It would be even worse if he was pitying her now. She was his matchmaker, not someone who would feel jealous…or at the very least, not someone he should know might feel some jealousy. Her emotional upheaval was not his problem.

"You'd better have a more positive attitude than that," Adel said, tapping his arm. "Come on. Let's go say hello. Just be your charming self, and you'll be fine."

That sounded confident, didn't it? She was actually quite pleased with her own deportment today. She was getting better at acting the part of a confident matchmaker. They started off in the direction of the lawn dart game.

"I'm not sure I'm usually very charming," he said, leaning down so that his words stayed for her alone.

"Hogwash," she said. "You're perfectly charming with me."

More than charming. He could make her breath stop in her chest with one of his drilling looks. He'd managed it last night in the kitchen.

"That's different," he murmured.

She looked up at him. "Is it?"

"Entirely." He met her gaze, but he didn't say anything else. They were too close to other people now anyway to keep their conversation private, and Adel let out a shaky breath. Was he toying with her? Or was she just too susceptible to every little flirtatious thing he said?

He *was* charming. And if this was the way he could make his own matchmaker feel, if he decided to, he could sweep any woman he wanted off her feet.

"You don't have a lot of time left, Jake," she said quietly. "Don't forget that."

"I know." He sounded irritable.

"Then use some of the charm you've laid on me, and find yourself a wife," she said. "There's only so much I can do unless you put in some effort, too."

Naomi smiled and waved when they approached, and both Verna and Sarai looked up, too. Verna suddenly smoothed her dress and her fingers fluttered up to her hair and her *kapp*, so it would seem that she'd already knew why Adel would be bringing Jake around. Sarai just smiled in a friendly way and put her hands on her hips.

"Hello," Adel said. "I wanted to properly introduce you to Jacob Knussli."

"Hello." Verna put her hand out and he shook it. "We don't actually need an introduction. We've talked a few times."

Jake looked mildly confused.

"I'm Verna. I make the lemon meringue pie you liked," she said.

"I thought you were Abram's wife—"

"No, that's Amanda." Verna's cheeks reddened.

Jake gave her an apologetic smile. "I'm sorry about that. I had just filed you away as married. You'll have to forgive me."

"Oh…" Verna's smile was back. "It's nice to see you again, Jacob."

"Call me Jake."

"Jake." Verna smiled, then she turned toward the younger woman next to her. "This is Sarai."

"Hi." Sarai didn't offer her hand to shake, but she did smile. "You're the subject of a lot of gossip, Jacob Knussli."

"Am I?" Jake turned and shot Adel a pretend look of alarm. "I should fix that."

Adel rolled her eyes and gave him a rueful smile. Yes, he'd be just fine here.

Sarai nodded toward the lawn darts. "Are you any good at this game?"

"Probably not," he said.

"Well, you can't be any worse than me," Sarai said, and she eyed him for a moment. "Besides, I like winning, Jacob Knussli."

"You should call me Jake, too," he said. "It's what everyone calls me."

"No, I'll call you Jacob," she said. "If everyone calls you Jake, I want to be different. How old are you, Jacob?"

Adel felt her own face heat, then. She'd insisted upon calling him Jacob for quite some time, too, but for different reasons. It felt almost like treading upon her turf.

"I'm thirty-seven," Jake said.

"You look younger than that." Sarai smiled sweetly.

When Adel's gaze flickered toward her sister, Naomi handed her lawn dart to Jake.

"Take over for me," Naomi said. "And don't hurt yourself."

Jake laughed and waggled a finger at Naomi. Then Adel and Naomi moved a little ways away to give the group more privacy.

"Sarai is downright flirting!" Naomi said. "And I've never seen Verna quite that forward with any man before. Did you plan that?"

"I couldn't have planned that if I tried," Adel said. "But I think having something social to do while talking is at least an easier way to start things. The formal sit-downs have a way of squashing Jake's more relaxed nature. He flirts better when he's relaxed."

"You'd know about that." Naomi nudged her arm.

"No, I'm being serious. Look at him! He's downright charming."

"And you're…okay with this?" Naomi asked softly.

"I'd better be. If this works, he'll have his wife and his farm. That's the plan."

"You're better for him than either Verna or Sarai would be," Naomi said.

Adel watched as Sarai took her turn tossing the lawn dart. It was Jake's turn next, and his landed right in the middle of the hula hoop. But instead of looking toward Sarai, who was groaning because he'd virtually just won, Jake's gaze turned toward Adel, and he mouthed the word *wow*.

Adel chuckled and gave him a thumbs-up.

"See?" Naomi said. "He's not trying to impress either of them. He's doing this for you."

Was he? Even with the beautiful, young Sarai right there, his gaze moved toward her. The thought made her stomach tickle. But no—she couldn't toy with this! This was Jake's future, and the farm that held his memories. He needed to make a choice, and she was only getting in the way.

"We should move farther away," Adel said. "Come on, let's get some food. I don't want to get in the way of him actually talking to them."

Naomi sighed, and they headed for the food table.

"How do you like being a matchmaker?" Naomi asked.

"I thought I'd like it," Adel said. "I'm not sure I do."

"Because you have to set Jacob Knussli up with another woman?" Naomi asked.

"Because meddling in anyone's love life is a bigger responsibility than I had previously appreciated," she replied. "Someone always gets hurt."

Her sister put her arm through hers. "I'm sorry, Adel…"

Adel hadn't meant herself when she talked about getting hurt, but maybe it applied, too. She sighed. They arrived at the food tables. Adel took some cut vegetables and dip, and for a moment, she just swirled a broccoli floret in the puddle of ranch dressing. She refused to look in Jake's direction.

"Are you okay?" her sister asked.

"It'll be fine," Adel said. "Let's just give Jake some space so he can apply that charm to the right woman."

"*You* might be the right woman," Naomi said.

"Not me!" Adel said irritably. Why would no one listen to her when she said that?

Jake finished the game of lawn darts and when he looked around for Adel, he didn't see her. He chatted with some friends from his boyhood, and listened to them talk about family life. Noah and Thomas Wiebe were both married now, and Thomas was talking about a little girl from Haiti. He already had a daughter from a relationship with an *Englisher* woman, and he and his Amish wife had adopted a little boy named Cruise, who followed Thomas around like a shadow.

Thomas scooped up the boy into his arms.

"We're praying about adopting another child," Thomas said. "The child we're praying to bring home is a little girl who was born in Haiti, but she's in America now. She's four years old, so she's very close in age to Cruise. They'll make good playmates. We've seen pictures of her, and she's really cute. Patience and I are looking forward to meeting her soon. Her name is Fabienne."

"From Haiti?" Jake asked in surprise.

"*Yah.* It's a different culture, but she's still a little girl in need of a loving home." Thomas looked a little defensive. "The adoption workers are quite impressed with our determination to raise our *kinner* with the memory and pride of the family they were born to while still giving them an Amish life."

"I didn't mean to offend," Jake said quickly.

"I lived English for a long time, so I can appreciate diversity. Truly."

"These adoptions between very different cultures might not happen often, but it does happen," Thomas said. "Plus, there was Micah Graber down in Indiana who married an Amish convert originally born in the Philippines. She speaks perfect Pennsylvania Dutch now, as well as a few other languages. And I've met some men who had adopted *kinner* from different cultural backgrounds. Love is what makes all the difference. *Gott* is calling us Amish to grow in new and deeper ways. I'm sure of it."

"Amen," Jake said quietly.

"If she comes to us, Fabienne will be raised Amish," Thomas went on. "But we will never take her heritage from her. Ever. *Gott* created her as a full person, and we'd never take a piece of her away."

"That's amazing," Jake said. "I have heard of that happening…but no one I knew personally."

"Well, you haven't met Patience," Noah interjected. "She's the heart of their home, in every way."

"That's the truth," Thomas said quietly. "Patience already wants to learn how to do her hair in braids, she's so certain that *Gott* will bring Fabienne to us."

"If her heart is in it, I'm inclined to believe it, too," Noah said with a somber nod. "*Gott* seems to tell a woman things he doesn't tell a man. So it's a wise husband who listens to her."

"That's some marriage advice for you," Thomas said. Cruise wriggled to be let down and Thomas set him on the grass. The boy headed off in the direction of the women who were chatting under a peach tree.

"Noah's wife is expecting their second baby," Thomas added.

"*Yah.*" Noah nodded proudly and pointed in the direction of a largely pregnant dark-haired woman sitting on a blanket. A toddler boy was playing with some sticks in the grass next to her, and Cruise joined his cousin and aunt. "We're having another boy. Samuel will be a big brother."

Thomas shaded his eyes and looked over at a pretty blonde who was also looking at him. Thomas pointed to where Cruise had gone with Noah's wife, and the woman smiled and nodded. She had a little girl at her side wearing an exact replica of her own dress and apron.

"That's Patience," Thomas said. "And that's our daughter, Rue, with her."

Their connection, even across the yard, as they parented in unison, was impressive to witness.

"So listen to your wife…any other advice?" Jake asked.

"Choose the right woman," Noah said quietly. "Even if she seems like the least appropriate choice. If she's the right one, it makes all the difference. I would know. Eve wasn't the appropriate choice for me, but I just knew on a bone-deep level, you know? And so did she. There was really no keeping us apart. At every turn, *Gott* seemed to be tugging us together."

Jake nodded slowly. "It's what I'm looking for."

But would he find it in time? Because the one woman who'd caught his attention like no other was in no way interested in him. She saw him as her client, nothing more.

The rest of the afternoon slipped away with a lengthy hymn sing, and the sun sank below the horizon. A bonfire crackled from a firepit on the far edge of the yard where the older kids and teenagers were roasting marshmallows. Jake had seen Adel around, but she'd kept a bit of a distance from him, giving him nothing more than an encouraging smile when he stopped to talk with any woman who happened to be single. Word was out, it seemed. Jake was in want of a wife, and there was a farm in it for the woman who took him on.

But Jake was tired now. Deeply tired. He didn't have it in him to make nice with any more women this evening. He was ready to head back to the bed-and-breakfast, but he'd driven Adel and her sister out to the hymn sing, and he'd have to drive them back.

He spotted Naomi over with Verna and Sarai, and he didn't dare go back over there. Sarai had developed a keen interest in him, and while she was incredibly pretty, she was too young for him. That was it, wasn't it? That was why he just couldn't summon up the determination to talk to her more seriously... He needed a woman more like Adel—his age, with some life experience, and beautiful. He needed to find what Thomas and Noah had found.

He headed away from the people and toward the farmhouse. He just wanted some space for a few minutes. He had a lot to think about. The sound of some men singing together surfed the breeze, and he strolled out toward the house, meaning to head toward the buggies.

But as he passed the side door, it suddenly opened and Adel stepped out. It took her a moment to see him in the shadows where he stood, and she startled.

"Oh, Jake!" She laughed breathily, and there was something about the way she said his name that warmed him from the inside.

"Sorry to scare you," he said. "I was just... taking a walk."

She hesitated on the step.

"You've been avoiding me," he added.

"I've been giving you space," she said. "You needed to talk to women on your own."

"Well, I've done that," he said. "Do you want to walk a bit?"

He'd missed her this evening—knowing she was around somewhere, but never able to get close enough to her to talk or just take a rest by her side.

"Sure," Adel said, coming down the steps. "You can let me know how it went."

He looked down at her. He didn't *want* to talk about other women... That wasn't helpful with his matchmaker, was it? They strolled together in the direction of the buggies, away from the murmur of voices, the laughter of children, the singing of those men who'd taken up a new hymn... The evening was warm, and he felt the reassuring brush of her sleeve against his arm.

"Well?" she prodded. "Tell me."

"Uh—" He looked toward the fire flickering in the distance. "Verna is very nice, again, but no spark."

"Okay," Adel said. "I expected that, after watching you a bit. But what about Sarai? You liked her."

"She's…great. I mean, she's pretty, she's fun, she certainly seems to like me—" He looked down at Adel and she quickly looked away. "But no." "No?" She looked back. "Really?"

"She's too young."

"She's twenty-five."

"*Yah*, but she's very perky," he said.

"She's happy. She's upbeat." Adel shook her head.

"She's not right," he said. "I want someone older—our age. I want someone who's experienced some life, who could understand me a little better."

"You didn't have a list when we started, and now you're getting a whole lot harder to please, Jake." She sounded annoyed, and he smiled in the darkness.

"Adel, I want her to be more like you." He wouldn't have dared to say it in the light of day, but he felt Adel freeze. Was she holding her breath? "Adel?"

"Like me?" she whispered.

He caught her hand. "You're quite wonderful, you know."

Adel looked down, and he stepped closer to see her better in the darkness that was illuminated by a sliver of moon and a splash of stars.

"You're smart," he whispered. "And you've seen things—you know that life is hard. You're funny, too. You're fun to be around, and—" He swallowed. "You're beautiful."

She looked up then, and her face was so close to his that he could feel her breath tickle his chin. He ran his hands lightly down her arms.

"You're supposed to choose one of them," she whispered back.

"Adel, you understand me," he said quietly. "You see me as…as a man. As a person. Well, I see you the same way."

"As a man?" Her lips turned up into a teasing smile.

"Hardly." He chuckled. "But I understand you."

"Prove it." She lifted her chin in a sort of challenge.

"All right." He caught her hand in his. "You got married young, and you didn't marry for love. You married for respect, and the love came later. You trusted our Amish way of life to deliver you a beautiful future, and it did deliver. So our ways are a safe haven for you. Am I right so far?"

"Surprisingly accurate," she said softly.

"Okay," he said, encouraged. "Well, you're also scared. Because when you got married, you trusted your *daet* to steer you right, and you don't have that anymore now that he's passed. I think you've been looking to the bishop to provide you with that kind of insight these days. So you're widowed, and you appreciate all that your marriage provided for you, and you're digging your heels in. You don't want to risk what you've already gotten."

Adel's breath quickened. "You're right. I don't want to risk it."

"I think I understand you pretty well, given a short amount of time," he said.

"*Yah*, but I'm the one who's supposed to understand you," she said. "And you won't just do things the normal way, Jake."

"I like my way better." He squeezed her hand. "Besides, it's only fair."

She dropped her gaze.

"You were a puzzle to me before," he went on. "But I get you now."

"Not many people do," she said, and he felt a rush of satisfaction at that. She wasn't the typical Amish person, either. And maybe that was why he felt so drawn to her.

"But you've never experienced *this* before," he whispered.

"Experienced what?" She looked up. She really hadn't put it all together yet?

"Attraction," he said softly. "The natural kind that just pops up between a man and woman sometimes when they're both free and single. You haven't had this."

"I was married," she said with a dismissive little laugh.

"Yah." He nodded. "You were, but it didn't start like this. That's what I'm saying. You aren't in control of these feelings between us."

"I'm not *supposed* to be feeling this," she said softly.

"Maybe not." He touched her cheek. "But I'm glad you do. It's not just me, then. There's something here that we both feel..." he licked his lips "...and I'm thinking about kissing you."

She didn't answer, but her eyes glistened in the moonlight, and he thought he could make out a soft blush on her cheeks. Her lips were so close, and when he touched her chin, tipping her face up just a little bit, she leaned toward him ever so subtly, and he threw all his reserves to the wind and lowered his lips over hers. Her lips were soft, and her hands pressed gently against his chest, his own heartbeat thudding against her touch. She sighed and leaned into his arms. She was warm, and soft, and she smelled ever so faintly of baking. She felt like happiness and moonlight all wrapped up together. This kiss was exactly what his poor, battered heart needed.

Adel suddenly pulled back, and she pushed against his chest. He released her, taking a surprised step back.

"We can't do that," she breathed.

"Oh…" He'd offended her. He didn't mean to. "We're both single," he added.

"That might be reason enough in the *Englisher* world, but you should know better here!" She touched her lips with the tips of her fingers. "What if someone saw us?"

Jake looked around. There was no sign of anyone around. Over by the bonfire, there was an eruption of laughter with the teenagers as two boys tussled over something they were too far away to make out.

"Adel…" She turned to look at him. "There *is* something between us."

"Maybe so," she whispered. "But this isn't part of my plan. This isn't how it's supposed to work."

"Sometimes things go differently than you planned," he said.

"We need to snap back into reality. You don't have time for this!" She met his gaze earnestly. "You have a matter of days now to find a wife. *You don't have time.*"

And she was right, of course. This would be a waste of time if what he felt for her wasn't so overwhelming. But he couldn't seem to look at another woman seriously now that he'd had some time with Adel…and now that he'd kissed her?

"We have to stick to the plan," she said, and he could hear a note of pleading in her voice. "We'll be glad we did when this is over. I'm sure of it."

Was she really so sure? Because he wasn't. Of all the women he'd met today, the only one to stick in his heart was his matchmaker, and she resisted every effort to get closer to her.

Chapter Eleven

The buggy rattled over a dip in the road as they headed back toward the bed-and-breakfast. Jake had the reins, and Adel sat between him and her sister, Jake's solid bulk on one side of her, and her sister's softer figure on the other. Jake moved his leg so that his knee touched hers, and she was sure it wasn't intentional. They didn't have much room with three adults squeezed into the front of one buggy, but all the same it reminded her of the feelings she shouldn't be feeling for him.

What would people say if they saw her kissing the single man she was supposed to be matching up with another woman? Her reputation would be crushed, and there would be no coming back from that. She couldn't take chances like that... This wasn't the kind of woman she was!

But we're both single... His words replayed in her mind. She wasn't doing anything sinful or wrong if she explored a future with another equally single man. Still, she wanted to be a respected woman who could provide wisdom, insight and possibly even arrange a marriage match for people. People with responsible positions in the community had to be more careful than others. They had more to lose and further to fall. Women would look to her for guidance and for a good example.

"Sarai seemed very interested in you, Jake," Naomi said, looking over Adel toward Jake.

"Yah," Jake said. "I know."

"She's a nice young woman," Naomi said. "She's got a good reputation around here, too. She's living with her grandmother right now to help her out with the garden and the house. She's been taken driving by a few hopeful young men, but she isn't courting anyone right now."

"Yah?" Jake's voice sounded tight.

"She cooks well, too," Naomi went on brightly. "And she's very pretty, isn't she— Ouch!" Naomi wriggled. "What was that elbow for, Adel?"

The buggy went over a bump and Adel pitched to the side.

"Sorry," Adel said meekly. "That was an accident."

At least it was…mostly.

Naomi shot her a mildly annoyed look. "She asked me to speak for her. I'm doing that."

"Verna is also a nice option," Adel said. Did they have to lean on Sarai quite so much?

"She's a nice option for someone else," Naomi replied. "Right, Jake? You said you wanted someone you had some spark with, and I didn't see anything between you and Verna. Unless I'm wrong there."

"No, there was no spark," Jake said, his voice low.

"Are you two having any luck finding that spark?" Naomi asked. Adel nearly choked, and her sister looked at her with exaggerated innocence for a couple of beats of silence. "Oh! I didn't mean it like that! Oh my… Things come out of my mouth all wrong sometimes. I meant finding someone Jake can feel that connection with."

Adel knew exactly what her sister had meant, and she was meddling. She glared at Naomi, but her sister pointedly avoided looking at her.

"I just think that some mutual attraction is important," Naomi went on. "I've seen some women get married with all the hope their hearts could hold, but you'd never know they were married in public because their husbands treat them like strangers. When two people really care for each other, and really feel honest attraction, it's impossible to hide."

Adel's breath caught. Was it really that impossible? It had better be somewhat possible to hide, because she had a reputation to maintain! She licked her lips.

"There have been young people who relied solely on attraction, got married and lived to regret it, too," Adel said.

"Yah..." Jake said.

Adel glanced over at him. What did that mean? She turned front again.

"What do you think, Jake?" Naomi pressed.

"I think that attraction is incredibly important," Jake said. "But a man with half a brain in his head wants both attraction and a good woman. It's a combination."

"Very smart," Naomi said.

"Attraction can develop over time," Adel said. "It did for me."

"What if it doesn't?" Jake asked, his voice low.

"If you work hard, treat her like the most beautiful woman in the world, and—"

"But what if even after trying very, very hard and treating her with respect and consideration, I still don't feel any honest, spontaneous attraction with her?" he said, cutting her off. "It's a possibility. We've all seen couples like that. When you want to kiss a woman, it comes from a different part of you—it isn't about duty."

That kiss… The way he'd held her, the way his lips had moved over hers… She could have stopped him. She *should* have stopped him. How could she recommend him to another woman who'd trust her to guide them straight, all the time knowing she'd been kissing Jake out by the buggies!

"Anything is possible," Adel said. "It's true—it's possible to choose a woman you'd never develop those deeper feelings for. But so is a buggy accident, or a lightning strike, or a house fire, or a flood… We take a step forward in faith that *Gott* will protect us and smooth the path. That's all we can do."

"Is it?" Jake looked down at her meaningfully. "Is it really *all* we can do?"

Adel's breath caught in her chest, and this time she elbowed Jake in the side. This was not a conversation to have in front of Naomi, and she had a feeling he was about to open up.

"As your matchmaker, it's my best recommendation," she said.

But the warm, agonized look he gave her left no confusion about how he felt. She could only hope that her sister hadn't seen it.

When they turned into the drive, Jake straightened his back. "I should go back to my own farm tonight."

And she felt a sudden tug in her heart. She'd upset him. Something had happened tonight that never should have, and he was going to leave. They needed a little more time just to set their balance right again.

"If you have food there," Adel said.

He didn't answer. He seemed to be considering.

"Jake, have another night here," Adel said, softening her tone. "I'm sorry if I was arguing with you. The farmhouse is fumigated, but you don't have your kitchen stocked or anything. You don't need to make anything harder on yourself." She looked at her sister. "Don't you think, Naomi?"

"Of course," Naomi replied. "You can't go back without food in the cupboards."

"I appreciate that," he said, his voice low. "I'll take care of the horse and buggy tonight. You two can go inside."

Did he guess that Adel might offer to help? Because she would have.

"I still feel a little bad, considering you're our guest," she said. It was a token resistance.

"I'm a whole lot more than a guest, aren't I?" he asked, and irritation flashed in his eyes.

She looked up at him and felt her cheeks heat. "Thank you, all the same."

When he reined in in front of the house, Adel followed her sister out of the buggy and dropped down to the ground. Then he carried on toward the stable. Adel stood there for a moment, her heart pounding.

"I think he's a whole lot more than a guest at this point, too," Naomi said, fishing the key out of her bag and heading toward the side door.

"Naomi, you need to stop that!" Adel followed her sister inside and shut the door firmly behind her. "He's my client! And I know that might be laughable to you, but I have a reputation to consider here!"

Naomi lit the kerosene lamp, and then turned toward her. "I saw you kiss him."

Adel's heart nearly stopped in her chest. "What?"

"I was coming to find you because I was tired and wanted to head home. I was hoping you were ready to go."

Adel swallowed. "I—" But she had no words. She couldn't defend herself.

"Adel," Naomi said quietly. "I'm not trying to shame you. I've been saying from the start that you're a good match for him."

"What kind of matchmaker would I be, taking him for myself?" Adel asked weakly.

"A terrible one," Naomi said bluntly. "But you'd also be married again, and happy."

"I am happy," Adel said curtly. "I know what I want, Naomi, and handsome as he is, he's a risk. He's asking what happens if the woman he marries doesn't end up sparking his romantic interest. Well, I have deeper concerns than that! What if I did allow myself to feel this, and the man I marry ends up being without any community respect? I'd go from the deacon's widow who everyone looked to for advice and wisdom, to being…married and nothing more."

"Married and nothing more? Marriage is a blessing all its own. If I could find the right man, I'd be honored to be married." Naomi glanced at her sister. "He's likeable, Adel. People are already accepting him back."

"*Yah*, but you know as well as I do that a woman's position in this life is reliant upon her husband's. I married a good and decent man in Mark. I loved him. I worked hard in our marriage, and I earned respect. I *earned* every ounce of that respect! It wasn't easy marrying a man so much older than me, but I did it, and I'm not giving up what I earned."

"Who's to say you'd give up respect? You might earn more of it. But let's say you are right. You wouldn't give up respect? Even for love?" Naomi asked softly.

Love... That was a heavy word that she didn't like to toss around lightly.

"He's a rebel at heart," Adel said. "I think that's all this is. I'm an inappropriate choice, so he sets his sights on me. And I don't need a rebel husband! I'd rather be a respected woman who can do some good around here than a married one whose time and effort are focused on maintaining a struggling relationship with someone who I only had one thing in common with—attraction."

Adel saw a bobbing lantern outside. Jake was coming back in.

"No more talk about this," Adel said. "Jake can't know what you saw, okay? And please, Naomi, don't breathe a word to anyone!"

"I won't," Naomi said. "But if you don't want him for yourself, you'd better be a whole lot more careful. Stop letting it get personal.

Don't go for walks with him. He's feeling this—I can tell."

So could Adel, and she rubbed a hand over her eyes. "I'll do better."

Jake came out of the stable when his horse was settled into the stall for the night, and he sucked in a chest full of fresh night air. He had been saying too much in front of Naomi, and he was kicking himself for it now. What he needed was some time alone with Adel to hammer this out. Because that kiss hadn't been a mistake—it had been honest—and he wasn't sorry for it. She'd leaned into his arms, and she'd kissed him back, and he'd felt a connection with her that he'd never felt before.

This was real—and she could reject him as was her right, but she couldn't claim it hadn't been real.

When Jake came into the house, he found Adel and Naomi in the kitchen. Naomi cast him a tired smile.

"I'm turning in," Naomi said. "Have a good night, Jake. I hope I didn't offend you with taking too much interest in finding you a match."

"It's fine," Jake said with a shrug. "I mean,

I am looking for a wife, right? Don't worry about it."

Naomi headed up the stairs, and Adel reached some cereal boxes out of the cupboard and put them down on the table in preparation for the next morning.

"Adel," he said quietly.

Adel turned toward him, her cheeks pink.

"You kissed me, too," he said.

The color in her cheeks darkened and she shot him an annoyed look. "That's not what you should be telling me."

"I don't care what I should be telling you. I'm telling you the truth," he said. "If you hadn't been feeling it, too, you would have smacked me."

She was silent.

"At least I think you would have…"

"*Yah*, I would have." She sighed. "That's why I'm embarrassed. I did feel it, too."

"Okay, well…good." Again, it was likely the wrong thing to say, but he was feeling frustrated. None of this was coming together the way it was supposed to. He was supposed to be courting another woman—*any* other woman!

"We need to be a whole lot more careful," Adel said.

Overhead he heard the squeaking of floorboards. "But I meant what I said in the buggy. We have something honest and spontaneous between us, and that doesn't actually come around very often. I just wanted to say that."

"The spontaneous part is why we have to be so careful," she said. "I agree—we do feel something. It's my responsibility to keep this professional, and I've let you down there."

"I wouldn't blame you entirely," he said with a joking smile. "I have worked pretty hard to figure you out."

She smiled faintly. "You have." Then she sobered. "But for me, this isn't about attraction. This is about following the path I believe *Gott* has set me on."

Adel was serious, and he could feel her firm resolve. Jake's joking evaporated and he took a step closer. "I'm the man here. It's on me. I won't overstep with you again."

"Okay." She sucked in a wavering breath. "I'd better get to bed."

He longed to close that distance between them, even if only to hug her, but that wouldn't help either of them. She turned toward the stairs. It was time for him to get to bed, too.

Jake closed the door behind him and headed into the little guest suite. He'd made his bed this morning, but it looked straighter than the way he'd left it, and there was a single chocolate left on his pillow like every other night. He picked it up and smiled faintly.

This was just a professional gesture, but he couldn't help but wonder if it was Adel who had left it there.

He unwrapped the foil, popped it into his mouth and sank onto the side of his bed.

I'm messing this up, Gott, he prayed silently. Were these the *Englisher* years coming back in his instincts, or had he always been this way? He liked to think that if he'd spent less time away from home and more time living Amish, he'd be a better man by now. Maybe he'd even be good enough to earn Adel's full respect and to have her take him seriously as a marriage candidate. The problem, in part, was the deadline. Maybe if he didn't have to act so quickly, he could make her see how right they were for each other.

Could he really marry another woman, feeling the way he did about Adel?

He opened his Bible at random, looking for some comfort. His eyes fell on a verse he hadn't seen in a very long time: *Keep thy heart with all diligence; for out of it are the issues of life.*

From *Gott*'s lips to his ears. Jake had to stop this now. Adel wasn't interested in a future with him, and he had a farm to consider. Maybe she was right and his self-control was more important than his emotion. Perhaps that was the making of a man, and he needed to grow before he would be husband material for a woman like her.

But time wasn't on his side.

"*Gott*, show me the right woman," he prayed aloud. "And help me to let Adel go."

The next morning, Adel stood at the kitchen sink drying the last of the breakfast dishes. She'd made a big breakfast—eggs, fried potatoes, sausage, cinnamon buns and some dry cereal, as well. Jake had eaten heartily before heading back to his farm to start chores, and now she stood in her quiet kitchen, listening to the soft ticking of the clock.

Today, there were no scheduled visits from tourist groups, and it would be a good time for Adel to sit down and balance the books. Yet, her mind kept going back to her current job of finding a wife for Jake. There had been some good options for him at the hymn sing last night, but he hadn't been able to think about them because he was blinded by what he felt for her.

If Adel truly cared about Jake's happiness, then she would step back and give him the chance to find a woman who wanted what he had to offer.

Like Sarai. She was almost everything he wanted, just a little younger than he'd hoped. But she was a grown woman, and no one else would worry about that age difference. While Adel had felt some jealousy at the thought of Jake with Sarai, that wasn't Sarai's fault. Adel would feel that with any woman he chose, and that put the responsibility squarely on Adel's own shoulders.

"I should go visit Sarai and talk to her a little bit about what she wants in a husband," Adel said.

"What's that?" Naomi popped her head in from the other room.

"I said, I should talk to Sarai…see if I can make that match for Jake," Adel said.

"He said he didn't want Sarai, though," Naomi said.

"Do you believe him?" Adel asked. "Sarai is sweet, bubbly, fun, full of personality…and of all the women he's met so far, she's the one he seemed to hit it off with the best."

"Maybe so," Naomi agreed, leaning against the doorjamb. "But if he isn't interested in her, then all you're doing is setting that poor girl up for disappointment. She really liked him."

"But him not being interested might be my fault," Adel said. "And if that's the case, I owe him a proper match, don't you think?"

"You do owe him a proper match," her sister agreed.

"And if we don't hurry up, he'll lose his farm."

"It's his farm to lose," her sister said quietly.

Adel pressed her lips together in frustration. Maybe it was his farm to lose, but he'd already been held away from home by gossip passed along by his cousin, and if he had lifelong regrets after losing the farm because his brain had been addled with thoughts of *her*, she'd never forgive herself.

"I'll talk to him about it tonight," Adel said. "He told me this morning before he left that he's coming back for one more dinner with us. But you're right. I can't plow ahead without his consent. It would be wrong, and I don't want Sarai hurt for nothing."

Outside, Adel heard hooves on the gravel and she leaned forward to look out the window. A buggy had turned into the drive, but Adel didn't recognize the driver. She was slim and pretty, and she held the reins with confidence.

"Who is it?" Naomi asked, coming up beside her. They both watched the woman drive past their line of sight, and then exchanged a look. "Do you know her?"

"I don't," Adel replied. "But we'd best go say hello."

Naomi went and opened the side door while Adel washed off the table and got a kettle started on the stove. A couple of minutes later, Adel heard Naomi's voice chatting cheerily, and then both came inside.

"It's a beautiful day," the visitor was saying. "Thank you so much for the offer of some tea. I'd love some."

"Hello," Adel said with a smile. "Come in. Sit down. You've met Naomi, but my name is Adel Draschel. You aren't from around here."

"No, I'm new here," she replied. "My name is Claire Glick."

She looked to be in her midthirties, and she had a pleasant smile and an easy way about her.

"Glick—any relation to our bishop?" Adel asked.

"*Yah*. Zedechiah is my second cousin. I've come to stay with his family for a few weeks while I get settled here in Redemption. He was the one who asked me to come see you—starting introductions, so to speak. He would have come along with me, but he said that he was busy and that you're so friendly, I shouldn't have any problems."

"That's kind of him," Naomi said. "And no, it's no problem at all. Are you moving here?"

"*Yah*. That's the plan. I'm not married yet, and it was time for a change of scenery, if you know what I mean."

Adel nodded. "We certainly do. You're very welcome here."

And it did explain why the bishop had sent this woman in their direction. She was single, looking to meet potential husbands, of the right age for Jake, and she seemed absolutely charming.

"So tell me about you," Adel said. "What are you looking for in a husband?"

She blushed. "No beating around the bush."

"Why waste the time?" Adel said, spreading her hands. "Besides, if the bishop sent you over, you already come well-recommended."

"Well, I'm thirty-two," Claire said. "Before

I left Ohio, I had my own business making baskets."

"Just baskets?" Naomi asked.

"There was a surprising market for them," Claire said. "A lot of home decor stores were stocking what they called 'rustic baskets,' and having ones that were handmade by an Amish person drove up the demand for them. I was supplying several local home decor stores, as well as gift shops."

"You must have stayed busy, then," Naomi said.

"*Yah.* Very. I even taught a class on basket weaving for *Englisher* women in the area. It proved very popular."

"*Yah?* They wanted to learn?" Adel asked.

"I honestly think they were mostly curious about me," Claire said. "They made terrible baskets, but they loved chatting with me. They'd ask me all kinds of questions. And I made a decent income from it."

This woman was smart, a hard worker, willing to take a few risks to get her own business running...

"Good for you!" Adel was impressed. "You certainly find a way to make a living."

"Well... You have to, don't you?" Claire glanced around. "Zedechiah was telling me that you run this bed-and-breakfast, just the two of you. Some fellow women in business."

"*Yah*, we do," Adel said. "It's a labor of love. We've been in business five years now."

"And every year is busier than the last," Naomi added.

They chatted about everything from business to Claire's connections in Ohio. While hearing Bishop Glick called by his first name felt wrong on all sorts of levels, she seemed to be very happy to be getting to know his family better. Apparently, her invitation to come try out life in Pennsylvania had come from the bishop's wife, Trudy.

"Claire, why don't you stay for dinner?" Adel said. "We can talk more while we cook. There is someone—" she swallowed, tried to bring the earlier cheer back into her voice "—there is someone I want you to meet."

"Oh?" Claire's eyebrows rose.

"He's very nice. I think you'll like him. No pressure. Just…meet him."

Naomi met Adel's gaze, and Adel saw sympathy in her sister's green eyes. Adel was doing the right thing. From what she could see, the bishop had found the perfect match for Jacob Knussli. She had all of Sarai's charms, and she was a more appropriate age for him, too.

Maybe *Gott* was moving here, and all of this was *Gott*'s will. When *Gott*'s people were truly blessed, He used them to be the answer of someone else's prayer.

Gott's path was a selfless one. Perhaps Adel was getting a lesson in just that.

Chapter Twelve

Jake's stomach rumbled as he unhitched his horse from the buggy next to one he didn't readily recognize. Did they have another guest at the bed-and-breakfast? Whoever the owner, this buggy was well-cared for, which couldn't be said for his uncle's. He paused, his gaze moving over the battered, peeling paint. Uncle Johannes hadn't taken care of his things, and the first thing Jake would do when he got the land put into his name was to buy a new buggy of his own that he could be proud of. And then he'd take proper care of it.

There were too many things his family hadn't properly cared for—including the ties that bound them. He wasn't much better, he had to admit. He shouldn't have accepted secondhand gossip as gospel truth, even though it gave him the excuse to take the easy way out.

Jake opened the gate for his horse to enter the corral, locked him inside and then headed back toward the house. Adel waited at the door for him, and when he came up the steps, she gave him a nervous smile.

"Hi," he said quietly.

"Hi." She smiled, and some color touched her cheeks. "How was your day?"

"Busy. I tagged some new calves, and there's a mare that has hurt her leg, so that took some time to get her settled in the stable where she won't be bothered..." It was a day on the farm, and it wasn't really what he wanted to talk about. He lowered his voice further to make sure his words were private. "I missed you."

She dropped her gaze. "You shouldn't—"

"It's true, Adel. I thought about you all day. I tried not to. I *prayed* not to. I still did."

She looked up at him, her eyes full of agony. Was she going through the same thing?

"Did I cross your mind at all?" he whispered.

"Of course!" She sighed, and kept her voice low. "All day long. But I realized today that I'm in your way. I'm not much of a matchmaker if I'm stopping you from finding a wife. Luckily, the bishop hasn't forgotten you, and he sent someone over for you. Someone... rather perfect."

Her voice caught at the word *perfect*, and he wondered how hard this was for her.

"Who?" he asked.

"Bishop Glick's distant cousin who is staying with him for a little while. She's very nice." She swallowed. "She's in the kitchen."

Another setup. Of course—that was why he was here, wasn't it? It was supposed to be, at least. But his heart dropped all the same.

"Okay," he said.

Adel was silent a beat, as if she wanted to say more, but then she seemed to steel herself as she stepped out of the way and gestured him inside.

"Claire," Adel said brightly, raising her voice to be heard. "This is Jacob Knussli. He's the one I was telling you about."

Claire was a pretty woman who looked close to his age. She had a ready smile that lit up her face in a rather nice way.

"This is Claire Glick. She's from Ohio."

Jake shook Claire's hand. She met his gaze easily, then gestured toward a coffeepot on the table.

"Did you want some coffee?" she asked. "I was about to get some cream."

"*Yah.* Thank you."

She was attractive, easygoing. They all chatted together as the final preparation was done on the meal, and when they all sat down, she was placed next to him, and Adel and Naomi seemed very engaged with each other.

He knew what Adel was doing—giving him a chance to talk to Claire. The more they chatted over a hearty meal, the more he liked her. She was a truly wonderful person. But every time he glanced over at Adel, his heart gave a little tug. Adel was special—there was no getting around it. But there was no opportunity to talk to Adel alone; she made sure of that.

Chatting with Claire didn't come with any of the nervous awkwardness he'd felt with meeting other women. If he wanted this match, he had a feeling it was falling into place rather nicely. Except no one had mentioned whether or not Claire knew about his need for a wife within a week. The time restriction was an important detail, but he was loath to bring it up for some reason he couldn't quite name.

Gott, is this the woman for me? he prayed.

Do I just have to ignore what I'm feeling for Adel and push past it?

That was what he needed to know. Because he'd prayed all day that *Gott* would wipe his heart clean of Adel to allow him to move forward, and *Gott* hadn't answered. Was Claire the woman he'd been praying *Gott* would put in his path? Because next to Adel, all of Claire's wonderful qualities dimmed, just like with every other woman he'd met. Except he was able to admit that Claire did check off every single box on his list of wifely requirements better than any other...even if it didn't feel completely right.

After dinner, Claire helped to clean up, and between the three women, it took very little time. Then Claire thanked them for the meal and said she'd best get back, as she knew she'd be missed. He imagined that Bishop Glick and his wife could manage without her for a single evening, but maybe it was Claire's way of breaking free. What did he know?

"I'll help you hitch up," Jake said. It was the polite thing to do.

As he headed outside, Jake glanced over his shoulder and found both Naomi and Adel watching him go. Naomi looked thoughtful, and Adel was hiding whatever she was feeling behind a pasted-on smile.

Jake worked quickly to hitch up her horse, and Claire helped with the buckles on the other side of the animal.

"It was very nice to meet you," Jake said.

"Likewise." She smiled, then paused. "Perhaps I'll see you again."

"I'm sure you will," he replied. "I'm around." And if he could get past his own stubborn heart, maybe he'd go talk to her more earnestly later.

"You own a farm around here, you said?" Claire asked.

"I'm inheriting it. It's a bit of a process," he replied. She'd brought it up, and now was the time to tell her about his need for a wife, if any. But he couldn't quite bring himself to do it. The words stayed stuck inside him.

"I understand." Claire smiled again. "I'd better get going. I have someone waiting for me."

That was the second mention of someone waiting for her, and this time it didn't sound like she was referring to the bishop and his wife. Perhaps she wasn't quite so single as Adel thought.

"Of course." He offered her his hand, and she got up into the buggy. "Drive safely."

She waved, and flicked the reins as she expertly pulled the buggy around. He stood in the drive, watching her go. He heard the screen door slam, and he looked over to see Adel come outside.

She'd taken off her apron, and her teal-colored dress brought out the pink in her cheeks. She was the kind of beautiful that made it hard for him to look away.

"That was a delicious meal, Adel," he said.

"Thank you." She crossed the gravel and came to a stop beside him. "You're always welcome to come for dinner, you know."

"Yah?" He smiled faintly. "I feel like you don't offer that for all your bed-and-breakfast guests."

"You've become more," she said softly.

More. Yes, they'd both become a lot more to each other, but naming it was difficult.

"I intended to pick up a few groceries before heading home so I could fend for myself again," he said.

She nodded, then looked in the direction of Claire's buggy, turning on to the main road. "Did you like her?"

He could hear the pain in her voice she was trying to cover.

"She's nice," he said.

Adel met his gaze. "You know what I'm asking."

"I do know what you're asking," he said. "But I don't know her. She's very nice. She's cheerful, charming, sweet… And there is someone she's eager to get back to. I highly doubt it's our bishop."

Adel frowned. "I'm sure she's single. Bishop Glick wouldn't have sent her over otherwise."

"She mentioned getting back to someone twice," he said. "If she doesn't have someone else, then maybe she was just eager to get away… I might not be quite so charming as you think."

Adel rolled her eyes. "You're perfectly charming. You're handsome, hardworking, easy to talk to—" Her eyes misted and her voice caught.

"I don't think she's interested," he said. At least it would make things easier if she wasn't.

"I know Bishop Glick better than you do," Adel said. "And he knows his relative better than you do, too. I talked with her for a long time before you arrived, and she's confirmed that she's single. Very single. She's moved out here to get to know other available men."

"Maybe the bishop told her about my time away," he said. "It puts some women off."

"Did you tell her about the farm?" Adel asked.

"No."

"I think you should. It would explain the speed that you need to move in this. There isn't time to court her properly, or visit her weekly for a little while. There just isn't *time!*"

"I don't think she's for me," he said.

"She's—" Adel shook her head. "She's perfect, you woolen-headed man! She's perfect! Can't you see that? She's your age, she's smart, she's funny, she's talented, she's got a mind for business, and she's just as delightful as Sarai is! She's *perfect* for you!"

"She's—" Jake took off his hat and slapped it against his leg. "She's not you!"

"No woman will be!" she shot back. "And you don't have time to be picky. I've found you several appropriate women, and you've turned them all down, save Delia. And I have a feeling you would have turned her down if she hadn't done it first! You need a wife. I've given you good options. There aren't any other women to choose from unless you want to move to the widows in their sixties and seventies! I've done my best!"

"I know," he said.

"Then make a choice already!" Tears welled in her eyes. "Because this is killing me!"

She dashed the tears off her cheeks.

"It's killing you?" he whispered.

"What do you think?" she asked, shaking her head. "I have to find a woman for you and see you *marry* her. I have to see her fall in love with you, and you do the same. I have to watch you build a home with someone else. I hate every second of it!"

So she was feeling this, too. Just as strongly as he was. Because he didn't want to choose another woman. He didn't want to build that home with a virtual stranger who would be ever so nice, but never quite fill his heart.

"Do you *really* want me to marry someone else?" he asked.

Adel stared at him, her heart hammering so hard in her chest that she could almost hear it. Jake stood so close to her that she had to tip her face up to look him in the eye, and a lump closed off her throat. She didn't trust herself to use words, so she shook her head.

"That's what I thought..." Jake gathered her up in his arms and his lips came down over hers. He pulled her in hard against him, and she instinctively grabbed handfuls of his shirt as she melted into his embrace. She didn't want him to marry someone else. She wanted him to stay like this—hers on some undeniable level. His kiss was slow, warm and heartbroken. It was like the evening just melted away around them, and nothing remained but the two of them and the soft whisper of breeze.

She'd been thinking about his kiss for a long time, and here in his arms, it was possible to forget about all her very good reasons to keep her heart walled off, how she needed to listen to *Gott*'s voice, not her own desires, and she believed He had given her a mission in life she shouldn't so easily discard.

With his strong hand splayed over her back, all she wanted were kisses like this one, and time alone where they were nestled away from everyone else with no questions to answer...

But this land of in-between could not last. If Jake wasted his time with her, he'd lose the land he longed to own, and eventually someone would come asking questions...

She pulled back, and Jake released her, but his gaze stayed locked on her face with a look of such longing that it nearly broke her heart.

"I don't want you to marry anyone else," she said helplessly, "but I can't marry you, either, so where does that leave us?"

"Why can't you?" he demanded. "We're both free and single! We'll run my farm. We'll figure it out."

He made it sound so simple, and it would be for the first few months. But she'd been married before. She knew how this worked. Ahead of them, beyond the wedding and the honeymoon period, real life was waiting for them.

"I'm not free!" She shook her head. "Not in the way you are. I'm tethered to a man's memory, and that's the only way I'll have the life I want."

"You can't change your mind about what you want," he said.

"I sacrificed for *years*!" Her voice shook. "I prayed and prayed while I was trying to have babies and I couldn't. I begged *Gott* to show me why He was denying me the one thing every other woman seemed to do so easily. And He did. He showed me a different kind of life where I was able to be so much more in my community because I had less to hold me back at home. And now, I have nothing to hold me back at home…and I can truly step into that role *Gott* showed me. I can't go against His will for me. I suffered for this, and if I give it up now, all that was for nothing!"

"Not for nothing," he said. "It would be a second chance at all those things you wanted."

"But it would be giving up the path *Gott* showed me," she said. "I saw what was possible… I just didn't know how much I'd have to give up. I can't bend at the first test put in my way. I have to stay true to the mission He's given me."

Jake looked at her miserably, silent. Adel looked over his shoulder toward the house, and there was no movement there.

"I've seen people rush ahead because of their feelings," she said. "And it doesn't always work out well! I've seen people get married and live to regret their choice. I've seen men choose a woman based on a pretty face or his physical attraction to her, but marriage isn't just about romance and whispering sweet things to each other. It's much harder than that. There comes a day when you have to *try* to do the romantic things that used to come so naturally. And when that day comes, you'll be stuck."

"I wouldn't be stuck..." he said. "I'd be grateful."

"And I'd be...a wife." She shrugged weakly. "That would be all. Just a wife. The bishop wouldn't come to ask my opinion. The other women wouldn't ask for my guidance. I wouldn't be free to spend my hours talking through a teenager's troubles, or helping a new wife adjust to the realities of marriage..."

"Why not?" he demanded. "I wouldn't stop you!"

"Because they wouldn't ask!" she shot back. "No one would ask anymore!" She swallowed against that rising lump in her throat. "I thought my future out. I had a plan that made me deeply satisfied with my life choices. It let me contribute to my community in a way I never could as a *mamm* with a houseful of her own *kinner*. *Gott* had bigger plans for me. I had embraced that. I can't just throw it aside now based on what I feel for you. Follow your heart, they say. But the Bible doesn't tell us to follow our hearts! It tells us to do what is right! Hearts can be disastrously wrong!"

"You don't trust that I love you?" he asked miserably.

Just like that, all her logical arguments blasted apart and her heart skipped a beat.

Her breath caught. "You love me?"

"*Yah*... I do love you. I know it's fast, but I can't get you out of my head. All I want is some time with you. Tonight, coming for dinner, I just wanted a quiet evening near you. Every woman I meet dims in comparison to you. I love you, Adel. And I might not be good enough for you, or stable enough, or respectable enough, but it's the truth."

He loved her...

"You are good enough..." she whispered. "But you need a wife in a matter of days, and if as your matchmaker I marry you myself, I will prove that I couldn't be trusted to help someone else, because I let those boundaries be blurred. I will prove that I can't be trusted with more."

"Do you love me?" he asked.

She looked into her own heart, at the tumultuous feelings inside her—her longing to be with him, her constant preoccupation with what he was feeling, what he might want... the way every part of her seemed to settle into bliss when he kissed her.

"I do," she breathed. "But I can't marry you in a few days, even if I could give up the path I'm on. I'd need more time, time to discern what *Gott* wants for me. And you need a quick marriage. My love right now isn't enough—don't you see? Your love isn't enough! You need something more solid than romantic love. You need your farm. So let go of your ideals of finding love, and find a wife."

"Even if you have to watch me marry her, and build a life with her?" he asked, tears misting his eyes.

"*Yah.* Even so. Get your farm, Jake. It's yours."

She'd made her choice a very long time ago, and while she'd never known how hard it would be, she would trust *Gott* to carry her through.

Her years of sacrifice could not just be heartbreak that had no meaning. If they didn't lead to something bigger, then all it was was pain…and she couldn't believe *Gott* would give her such heartbreak for nothing.

Jake nodded and took a step back. "I don't know if I can do it, Adel."

"Go home," she whispered. "Sleep on it. Pray on it. And choose the woman *Gott* shows you."

Claire, or Sarai…or even Lydia or Verna. Any of those women would make loving and devoted wives. Given time, he'd learn to love them dearly. They'd have *kinner* together, and raise their family. Soon, he'd forget that he felt anything more for Adel than simple friendship.

Jake needed a wife, and it could not be Adel.

Adel lay in her bed that night, her heart in pieces. She'd thought she knew what heartbreak felt like. She'd endured enough of it throughout her life. There had been the nights she'd begged *Gott* for a baby—just one—that would give her a little child in her home to love. She'd even looked around for an Amish child in need of a home, but somehow, *Gott* didn't open those doors, either. And there had been days that she'd sat in the silence of her own kitchen, wondering if she and Mark would ever feel that special connection that she longed to feel. Then, when Mark died, there had been entire years that she spent wishing she'd appreciated her time with Mark instead of longing for something more.

She knew what heartbreak felt like, and somehow none of it had prepared her for this.

Because she did love Jake. She loved him in spite of all her better instincts, but marrying him now would mean going back fifteen years. It would mean giving up all the growth in her community. It would mean giving up the respect that she longed for. She would just be a silly woman falling for a man and marrying him in a matter of days.

That wasn't who she was. If she ever did marry again, it would have to be done soberly, carefully and with lengthy prayer. Marriage was too precious and too difficult to enter into any other way. It would have to be done in a way her community could respect—not following her heart into a foolish leap.

Fifteen years ago, *Gott* had given her a greater calling. Jake needed a wife now. She couldn't do that. This couldn't be *Gott*'s will! So why did it hurt so badly to let Jake go?

Chapter Thirteen

The next day was laundry day, and Adel stripped down the guest room—Jake's room. His bag was gone, obviously, and the only remnant of him was the musky scent of his aftershave, and she stayed stock-still in that spot, inhaling it until she felt her heart would break.

"Stop it," she said aloud to herself, and she piled the sheets and towels into a hamper and carried it down to the basement where the gas-powered wringer washer was located. She did her best to focus on the work at hand, but alone with the laundry, she did stop and let the tears flow a few times. She loved him. That was the problem here. If she'd only kept her heart secure and been the professional matchmaker she was supposed to be, this would be fine. She could be happy for him.

But now, Adel had to stay true to her word and help the man she loved marry another woman, and that was going to be the worst punishment she'd ever experienced.

"*Gott*, it's my own fault," she wept. "But take away this pain! Give me the generosity to do my job!"

Jake deserved a loving wife…and she had to find a way to be the matchmaker for this marriage, because otherwise, she'd have to tell Bishop Glick exactly why she couldn't do this…and the bishop would never see her the same way again. Everything she'd worked for, the reputation she'd built and the bishop's faith in her would be forever shaken. All because she was silly enough to fall in love with her client.

Adel sniffled, wiped her eyes on the back of her hand and hauled the heavy laundry out of the washer and into a hamper. Overhead, she heard her sister's footsteps. Naomi was baking, and Adel didn't want her sister to know that she'd been crying. So she took an extra minute to dry her eyes on the edge of her apron, then started up the stairs with her heavy load.

"Oh, Adel…" Naomi said as Adel came up the stairs and into the kitchen. Her sister cast her a look of sympathy.

"What?" Adel asked, forcing some cheer into her voice.

"You've been crying."

"I haven't."

"And now, you've been lying," Naomi shot back.

Adel blinked back a fresh mist of tears. "I'm fine. I don't want to talk about it."

"What happened last night?" Naomi asked.

"Nothing—" She swallowed, hating to lie. "Okay, it's something, but it's private, and really, in the grand scheme, it's nothing that matters. It's fine. I'm just emotional."

"Private." Naomi cast her a hurt look. "It's not so private as you think. You're in love with Jake and you're too stubborn to marry him."

"I'm not stubborn!"

"But you are in love with him."

Adel rubbed her hands over her face. "*Yah... Gott* forgive me, I am."

"You don't need forgiveness for recognizing that the man *Gott* put into your path is perfect for you!" Naomi said.

Adel swallowed. "He's *not* perfect for me, but he will make another woman very happy."

"And you want that?" Naomi asked.

"No. I'm selfish. I'm in love with him. I want him to stay single and miserable right along with me, but I can't ask that of him. He'll marry someone, get his farm, and he'll be happy. I have to get over it."

"Easier said than done," Naomi murmured.

"I'll have to."

"Why is he not perfect for you?" Naomi prodded. "You love him. He loves you. When people are in that predicament, they get married. It's simpler than you think."

Adel shook her head. "I need more time. I can't marry him in a matter of days. I need to pray, to be sure that it's *Gott*'s will. I was so certain that He was showing me a different path, and now because of emotion that changes? I need time to be certain, and he doesn't have that. He needs a wife now."

Adel headed outside. She didn't want to discuss this anymore with Naomi. They were so different that her sister would never understand why her position in this community mattered so much and how she felt *Gott* had shown her a path she must faithfully follow.

The sheets were heavy, and it took a lot of muscle to get them up on the line and straightened out. She headed to the lawn, farther down the clothesline to take hold of the sheets and give them a good flap to get the wrinkles out when she heard a buggy on the drive. She turned and squinted into the morning sunlight, recognizing Claire from the day before.

Was she coming to see what Jake had said about her? Adel's stomach tightened. Claire was perfect, and it was very likely that *Gott* had worked on Jake's heart last night and he'd come with a similar request.

But when Claire pulled up at the house, Adel spotted a small boy on the seat next to her. He was all of three, wearing baby shorts and a pair of sandals. He had rumpled blond curls, and when Claire tied off the reins, he leaned into her arms as she gathered him up.

"Hello," Claire said.

"Hello!" Adel pushed back her own moodiness and forced a smile. "It's nice to see you again."

"Yah?" Claire lifted the boy toward her. "Would you grab him for me?"

Adel caught the little one in her arms and he looked at her in mild surprise. When Claire landed on the ground next to them, she took him back.

"This is Aaron," she said. "My son."

Adel blinked, and Claire's cheeks bloomed pink.

"Oh…" Adel swallowed. "Oh, you're widowed! I'd thought you'd said—"

"I'm not widowed," Claire interrupted. "I'm just a *mamm*."

"Oh…" Adel nodded a couple of times as those details solidified into her mind. "Claire, I didn't realize. I'm sorry about that. Hi, Aaron. You're a sweet little fellow, aren't you?"

He leaned his face into his mother's shoulder, and Adel felt a flood of sympathy.

"I know it seemed like I was coming yesterday for your friend Jake," Claire said. "My cousin explained it to me when I got back. Then it all made sense… And Jake is very nice, but I didn't really come to see you for that."

"You came to start getting to know people," Adel guessed. "And you were right to come. I'm so happy I got to meet you."

"I know that me being a *mamm* might change things," Claire began.

"No!" Adel shook her head. "Not a bit. Claire, my late husband was a deacon, and I've seen people through the hardest times of their lives. I probably understand better than most. Don't think for a minute that I'd judge you."

Claire smiled mistily. "Thank you for that. But… I didn't just come to meet people. I wanted to ask for a job."

Adel stared at her. "A job?"

"I'm a hard worker," Claire went on, her voice shaking just a little. "Like I said yesterday, I've run my own business that was successful, and I could bring that to your bed-and-breakfast. I could make some baskets to sell, maybe even do some classes for some *Englishers*. That might bring in more customers, and spread the word about your place. I'm quite good with marketing that way... Or I was. When I knew people. But it worked really well in Ohio..." She seemed to run out of breath.

Claire needed a job. This wasn't what Adel had imagined at all!

"I don't really have a lot of extra income for the bed-and-breakfast," Adel said.

"But, I can cook, I can clean, I can scrub floors. I can garden!" Aaron wriggled on her hip and she put him down on the ground. "I could take care of the horses, too. If—" Claire swallowed. "I know it's a lot to ask, but if you'd let me live here, on-site. I wouldn't take up much space. But I have Aaron, and that makes getting married a little difficult for me. And getting a job where I have to pay someone else to take care of him... Well, I can't afford it. But if I could keep him with me, that would be my solution. I'd work hard. You could give me just a little extra for money in my pocket, and…"

"So…just to be clear…you don't want to marry Jake in a few days' time?" Adel asked.

"I don't *know* Jake." Claire shook her head. "I can't marry anyone that quickly. I have my son, and I can't risk his happiness being the unwanted child in the home of a man I leaped into a marriage with. I'd have to be more careful."

"I understand," Adel said, and she looked at the woman with a new understanding. Claire wasn't interested in just any man, and beautiful as she was, she was no match for Jake's needs right now.

"I know you aren't looking to hire someone right now, but Zedechiah seemed to think that you might make room for me."

"I honestly thought he was sending you to me as your matchmaker," Adel admitted. "I'm just starting out as a matchmaker, and… I'm sorry. I jumped to conclusions."

Claire shook her head. "He actually told me about your late husband, and he said that you had the wisdom and perspective of a much older woman. He said that you'd been through so much that it softened your heart toward other people's pain, and of anyone in this community, he thought that you could understand my situation and…perhaps hire me."

Her pain had softened her heart… It was true! It had. Her loss, her struggles, her hardship had all worked together to show her just how reliant they all were on *Gott*'s grace and mercy. The bishop hadn't sent Claire to her because of her respected position here, or because of her matchmaking ambitions. He hadn't sent her because of Adel's experience with leadership among the women, or her late husband's position in Redemption. He'd sent Claire, a woman with a three-year-old boy born out of wedlock, to the Draschel Bed and Breakfast because of her ability to open her heart to a single *mamm*. Her previous marriage, her life experiences, had all factored into this, but it wasn't quite the way that Adel had anticipated. This wasn't about her husband's position, or her own… It was about her heart. The bishop was counting on her empathy…

Adel hadn't answered, and Claire plunged on. "I know it's a lot to ask. Maybe there isn't enough extra to pay someone, but with a place to stay and food to eat, and maybe I could find some extra customers for baskets, if you wouldn't mind me doing that on the side—"

"I'd pay you, Claire!" Adel burst out, breaking out of her reverie. "I wouldn't ask you to work for nothing. But if you'd be happy living here, that actually might work. Maybe what I could pay you would be enough that way."

"Oh." A smile touched her lips. "I'd be very happy to live here. I think I got along with your sister, as well."

"She likes you a lot," Adel said with a nod. "And so do I. I'll have to talk to her, of course, but I think we can sort something out."

Claire's face split into a smile. "Really?"

"*Yah.* I do." Adel nodded. "I love your idea of the basket-weaving classes, and you can definitely have your business on the side. We'll pay you for your work, and you can stay with us. We could use another pair of hands pretty much everywhere. And having your little one around will be a true joy. I promise."

Claire's gaze suddenly moved past Adel toward the garden and she startled. "Aaron! No!"

Claire rushed forward. The little boy had pulled leaves off a lettuce plant, and Claire scooped him up and turned back toward Adel, stricken.

"That happens when *kinner* are around," Adel said with a smile. "Would you mind picking that head of lettuce? We'll have salad tonight. No harm done."

But something new was sinking into Adel's mind. The bishop had come to her for advice because of her ability to understand others, and to sympathize. Mark had chosen her for that very reason, and Adel had assumed all this time that the community's respect for her had been because of her deacon husband. And maybe it had started that way, but somewhere along the line, the bishop had decided to send his single mother distant cousin *to her*. That showed just how much he trusted both her discretion and her sympathy. This was a member of the bishop's extended family who needed both.

He'd trusted her because of her heart.

And the bishop hadn't once suggested Jake for Claire, either, even though it might have solved Claire's problems… Adel's pulse sped up as she led the way up into the house.

She quickly explained Claire's situation to Naomi, and Naomi just nodded.

"I think we'd all work together very nicely," Naomi said. "Adel's the real owner, and she takes care of the finances, so if she says we can do it, we can do it."

Adel turned and looked out the window, her mind spinning.

Gott, is my reputation built on something deeper than my marriage to Mark? I've been so afraid to lose what I built, what I thought You wanted for me, but maybe it wasn't built so much as a gift from You. Maybe I've been trying to hold on to something with two fists that I wasn't in danger of losing...

"Adel?" Naomi said. "Are you okay?"

Adel turned and met her sister's worried gaze. "Who am I in Redemption? Am I the deacon's widow, or am I simply a trusted woman?"

"You're my sister," Naomi said with a confused shake of her head. "You're a business owner. You're certainly respected. You know that."

But that wasn't what Adel was looking for.

"My cousin said that you have a very unique and special ability to understand others' pain," Claire said quietly. "He called it a gift of the spirit."

Adel shot Claire a smile. "And *Gott*'s gifts don't just slip away, do they?"

"I don't believe they do," Claire replied.

Adel turned toward her sister. "That means it's not based on my marriage. At least not anymore." She nodded a couple of times.

Naomi seemed to connect everything in a heartbeat, because a smile suddenly spread over her face.

"You're going to marry him, aren't you?"

Adel felt her cheeks heat. "I don't know. We'll see. But I need to talk to him."

Claire looked at Naomi in confusion.

"I'll explain later," Naomi said. "Trust me, this is good. Now, is this little guy hungry? Because I have cookies!"

Adel let out a slow breath.

Gott, *I love him. I do! I need to be certain if this is from You, though.*

So if Jake is the man You mean for me to marry, then I'm sure he'll ask me again. And if he isn't for me, I'll let him ask for another woman—anyone. Claire even! That is how I'll know.

Jake had been meaning to go visit Alphie again for some time, and somehow, now that his fragile, unfounded hopes with Adel had been dashed, he felt like something needed to be properly sorted out in his life. And he couldn't face the thought of marrying another woman.

What do I do, Gott? he prayed. Because he'd felt hollowed out and empty ever since he'd left Adel's property. He loved her... It wasn't going to change, and *Gott* didn't seem to be giving him an easy way out. Was it that this farm wasn't meant to be his? After six months of working it alone, was *Gott* going to tell him to hand the land over to Alphie, after all he'd done to him?

Jake finished his morning chores, and he had a choice—clean out more of this old house and make it ready for a wife, or deal with the problem he'd been avoiding since his return. Somehow, Jake felt nudged in the direction of Alphie's hardwood flooring business in town. If nothing else, he could sort things out with his cousin, because family was family, and what were the Amish if they didn't have relationships?

An hour later, Jake parked his buggy behind the flooring shop, and he headed into the showroom. There were different styles of flooring, different types of wood, different polishes...all on display along the walls. For the moment, the store was quiet and empty of customers, and Alphie looked up from a book he was reading in mild surprise.

"Jake," he said. "Are you all right? You look awful."

Did he? If attraction was hard to hide, it seemed like heartbreak was even harder. He didn't have it in him to pretend everything was fine, either.

"I wanted to talk to you about the farm," Jake said.

"Your farm, you mean," Alphie replied with a good-natured smile. "How's it going? Do you need some extra muscle around there?"

"It's not mine yet. I'd have to get married in a few days to make that happen. I don't think I'll be able to do it."

Alphie closed his book, walked over to the front door and flipped the sign to Closed. Then he turned to face Jake.

"I didn't think you'd have any trouble there, honestly," Alphie said. "You seem to charm the women easily enough."

"Marriage is long," Jake said. "It's a life-time commitment. There is no room for error when choosing a wife…or a husband, for that matter. It takes more than charm."

For the right woman, at least.

"I know a few single women I could introduce you to," Alphie said. "I'll even put in a good word. One is named Delia—you know her, she lost her husband a couple of years ago. The other—"

"I've met them," he interrupted. "I've got a matchmaker, remember? And she's introduced me to every single available woman in Redemption she thinks is suitable for me."

"I see." Alphie blew out a breath.

"I have a matter of days before my time is up, and I don't have a woman lined up to marry me. I don't think I have it in me to keep trying, either."

"Are you telling me that the farm is mine?" Alphie eyed him uncertainly.

"Maybe."

"Don't give up yet," Alphie said. "I'm sure Johannes wanted you to have it. I'm sure of it. But he also wanted you married. And maybe this is the push you need to get you into a proper home with a wife of your own."

Maybe it was, but Johannes's plan had a flaw in it—Jake wanted more than a willing woman; he wanted a true, deep, abiding love he could count on.

"Why did Uncle Johannes set this up the way he did?" Jake asked, shaking his head.

"Just get married. Was it to humble me? Was it a joke?"

"I have no idea," Alphie said. "But I was as surprised as you were at how he lined things up in that will. Jake, you know you deserve this land. It would have gone to your father, if he'd outlived Johannes."

"I know."

"If it falls to me, maybe we can work out a deal. Maybe you can rent it from me and carry on like you have. Maybe you could just keep running it and we'll forget about any rent."

"Maybe." Jake sighed. But it still wouldn't be his. It wouldn't be left to his children, either. It would be another man's land. Could Jake live there like that?

"Or just get married!" Alphie said.

"That takes more time than I have!" Jake shot back. "You can't just waltz back into a community after fifteen years away and have people trust you! An Amish life is about community, and that's something that's built over time. I'm still pretty freshly back. Six months—what is that? It's a blink for people around here!"

"Yah..." Alphie nodded.

"I should have come back sooner," Jake

said with a shrug. "And I can't help but wonder why you never did suggest it."

"Because you didn't want to hear it," Alphie said, shaking his head. "You were full
of stories about your *Englisher* life and plans,
and you were so angry with your *daet* and
your uncle—"

"Which you helped to fuel," Jake said
curtly.

Alphie dropped his gaze. "It was stupid of
me. I'm sorry that I did that. I wasn't lying
to you. I told you the truth about what was
being said, but... My wife has since pointed
out that just because it was true didn't mean
it needed to be repeated. So I apologize for
what I did."

"Were you hoping to keep me away?" Jake
asked.

"No! I liked seeing you." Alphie looked
around himself. "I'm not an important man,
Jake. I... I thought you wouldn't want to keep
having those coffee chats with me if I didn't
come with information—some inside view
of things. I admired you."

"A man who'd jumped the fence?" Jake
asked, stunned.

"My older cousin, who was always better-
looking, smarter and much more charming

than I ever was," Alphie said. "I always had looked up to you. I didn't know I was holding you back. I feel terrible about it."

Jake heaved a sigh. "For all the good it's done me."

"Everything was harder for me than it was for you," Alphie said. "You charmed girls, and I had a tough time doing that. Even when you came back, women were looking at you, commenting on your good looks. Look at me! I'm short, balding and think of jokes ten minutes too late. I'm good old Alphie. No women ever looked at me like they look at you."

"Your wife does," Jake said.

"I had to put in time to get her, though," Alphie said, shaking his head. "I had to court my wife for two whole years before I could convince her to be mine. And before that, I had to build up a friendship with her, and wait while other boys took her home from singing. It was agony."

"But you got her," Jake said.

"With time. *Yah*."

"Is that the secret?" Jake asked. "Time?"

Alphie shrugged. "Some of us don't have any other choice. But I have to tell you, you won't find a more grateful husband than me. I *worked* for her."

Time… That might be the only way. Alphie hadn't had any other choice, but it had been worth it in the end. He'd gotten the girl he loved and he had a family of his own now. If Jake wanted the same thing, he wasn't going to be able to count on charm or good looks. The woman he loved needed more than that.

"If you inherit the farm," Jake said, "would you give me the chance to buy it from you?"

"Do you have the money for a down payment?" Alphie asked, squinting.

"I might have just enough," Jake said. "I might not have done much else worth noting over the last fifteen years, but I did save."

"*Yah*, I'd be willing to sell it to you," Alphie said. "And I'd make it a good, low price, too."

"Thank you, Alphie," Jake said, giving his cousin's shoulder a squeeze. "I appreciate that."

"Don't give up quite yet," Alphie said seriously. "You have a few more days. Just… don't give up."

A few more days wouldn't count for much with winning over Adel, but Jake had come to a realization that needed prayer.

Sometimes, the things that mattered most in life took time: paying off a mortgage, saving up a nest egg, gaining wisdom…and most importantly, winning a wife. Maybe Alphie was right, and Jake hadn't ever built up the patience that men with fewer charms had to develop. But it didn't mean that patience wasn't the virtue that *Gott* was requiring of him.

Good things took time.

And so did prayer.

Chapter Fourteen

After chores that evening, Jake's muscles ached, but it was the kind of tired that felt good. He'd prayed just as hard as he'd worked that afternoon. The animals needed to be tended to, the barn and stables needed to be cleaned out. The bottle calf needed to be fed, and then fed again. And all that time, he prayed.

Because he was getting ready to give up on inheriting this farm. Maybe he'd buy it instead, if Alphie would stay true to his word on that.

Jake looked across the rolling hills, the familiar fence lines, and toward the house that held so many memories. But the foundation his Amish upbringing had given him wasn't just a house, land or memories. It was a faith in *Gott* to guide him through the unknown.

A life of faith wasn't about clinging to what was rightfully his. It was about stepping forward into the future, and he wasn't going to marry some nice, hopeful but ultimately wrong woman. Not for a house, or a barn, or even all the memories this farm held.

Alphie had told him not to give up, but this wasn't giving up—it was growing up. Jake knew what he was going to do tonight—he was taking a shower, and then heading back to the Draschel Bed and Breakfast. He was going to sit with Adel and have a cup of tea. That was it. But he was coming back every evening for a cup of tea for as long as it took for him to marry her. She needed time—he didn't blame her. There was no rush, but he'd prove himself. If it worked for Alphie, maybe it would work for him. Because she already loved him...

And if Alphie had other plans for this land when all was said and done, Jake was going to call that number for the dairy farm, and get himself a job. He wouldn't be a landowner, but he'd be an honest worker, and he'd have other hopes for his future that included Adel at the very heart of them.

As he walked toward the house, he spotted a black buggy parked in the drive, and a form standing next to the side door. She was dressed in pink, and he knew her immediately. What was Adel doing here?

His first thought was that she'd come because she missed him—because he sure missed her! But that thought dissolved as he realized that more realistically, she was probably here to get his decision on which woman he chose. He picked up his pace and she started toward him, too, so that when they met, there was a fence between them.

"Hi," he said, and he reached over the rail and caught her hand. She squeezed his fingers in return.

"I came with—" She held up a basket in one hand. "It isn't even my baking. My sister made the muffins. But they're very good and I thought you might like some."

Jake grinned. "Thank you. *Yah.* I wouldn't turn them down." They were both silent for a moment, then he said, "I'm afraid I have to fire you."

"What?" She frowned.

"As my matchmaker. You're fired."

Her face paled. "You've met someone…"

"What?" That conclusion hadn't even occurred to him. He climbed over the fence and landed on the other side. "No, I didn't meet anyone. I'm giving this place up. I'm letting Alphie inherit it."

"Why?" she breathed.

"Because I know who I want to marry," he said, shaking his head. "And it isn't any of the women you've brought around. They're very nice. Very decent, and they all deserve someone who loves them dearly. In other words, not me."

"Where will you go?" she asked, and he saw tears mist her eyes.

"Alphie might let me run this farm for him for a while. He said he'd be willing to sell it to me, too, but I'd have to wait and see if he really meant that once all the paperwork puts it in his name. If I need to, I'll rent a room somewhere close by," he said. "I can apply for farming work around here. I have a lot of experience."

"So you're not leaving?" she asked quietly. "Not going back to the *Englishers*?"

"When I came back, I meant it. Adel, you can't get rid of me that easily," he said, dropping his voice so that she blushed. He liked the way he could make that happen. "I'm going to work hard. And I'm going to come visit you for a tea every evening I can manage it. I'm going to ask you for a piece of pie, too, so I do hope you'll make some."

"Jake, what are you talking about?" she asked, meeting his gaze.

"I'm talking about courting you," he said, "and doing it properly. You deserve a proper courting, and you deserve a man who can make you blush, and who will steal some kisses, and who'll wait for you, as long as it takes for you to be certain of me."

"But there wouldn't be a farm for you," she whispered.

"There'd be something better—a wife. Land doesn't make the home. A woman does. If I have to choose between a farm and your heart, there is no contest. I hope you'll be home tomorrow evening, because I'll be stopping by."

Adel laughed softly and shook her head. "You're saying you want to marry me that badly?"

"*Yah*, I am." He looked down at her soberly.

"And you think it'll take that long, do you?"

It was his turn to suddenly feel off-balance. What was she trying to say?

"It might... I'm willing to wait."

"And what if I'd come to a few realizations of my own?" she asked softly.

He held his breath as she continued.

"You see, I thought that I'd paid some

sort of painful bill for the respect I had, and maybe I did at first. But I found out recently that the bishop wasn't sending people to me because of my late husband. He was sending them to me because I could understand hard times and broken hearts. So maybe *Gott* was using that time to grow me, to teach me to be a better woman, to love my neighbors better than I ever could have before. It wasn't wasted, Jake. That's what I needed to see— those years weren't a bill paid for blessings now. They were a character grown, a heart molded… Not a minute of them were wasted, because *Gott* was working on the inside of me. So maybe it's time to stop paying that bill and learn how to accept a gift from Above."

"Am I that gift?" he asked, almost afraid to say it.

"*Yah*, Jake. You are. I'm sorry I was so stubborn." She shrugged faintly, and his heart hammered hard, his mind spinning to catch up. He was fully prepared for months of effort, for a lengthy explanation…

"Are you saying you'd marry me?" he asked.

"Is that a proposal?" she asked, and she seemed to hold her breath.

"The first of a hundred proposals that you'll

likely get from me," he said. "*Yah.* I want to marry you. I thought I was clear about that."

"Then yes." A smile broke over her face.

"Wait—" He put his hands on the side of her face, and looked down into her eyes. "Did you just say yes?"

She nodded. "Yes!"

He dipped his head down and caught her lips with his. He kissed her long and deep, and every bit of his heart went into it. He gathered her close, and the basket dug into the side of his leg, but he didn't care. When he finally pulled back, his mind had caught up.

"How much time do you need?" he asked. "You can have as much as you want. We can get married tomorrow, or we can get married next year. Whatever you need. Truly."

"Jake—" She smiled. "You need this farm, too. And I don't need any more time. But I'm afraid my matchmaking days are behind me, once I tell the bishop I'm going to marry you myself."

Jake barked out a laugh. "Adel, there are some very nice women in this community who deserve good husbands. I have a feeling you could do something about that."

Adel caught his eye and then she laughed. "I think I could."

"But as for you and me, we need to visit the bishop," Jake said. "We have a very quick wedding to throw together."

"Very quick," she whispered, and he couldn't think of anything better to say, so he pulled her back into his arms and kissed her all over again.

His heart filled with a bewildered, joyful swell. He was going to marry her... There wasn't a happier man on *Gott*'s green earth, he was sure of it.

Epilogue

Three days later, Bishop Glick stood with Adel and Jake in his sitting room, Adel in a new blue wedding dress, and Jake in his Sunday best. The banns hadn't been announced—there was no time. But the bishop and elders had agreed that his situation was a unique one, and they would announce the marriage instead of the banns, and it would be forgivable.

Naomi and Claire were present, as were Alphie, his wife and those three rambunctious *kinner* who kept trying to wander off into the kitchen, where Trudy had an array of food waiting.

But Adel didn't notice any of that. All she saw was Jake's warm gaze locked on her face as the bishop intoned the vows.

"Do you, Adel Draschel, accept Jacob

Knussli as your husband, to love, support, respect and take care of all the days *Gott* gives you?"

"*Yah*, I do," she said.

Jake gave her a relieved smile.

"And do you, Jacob Knussli, accept Adel Draschel as your wife, to love, protect, cherish and take care of for all the days Gott gives you?"

"Most certainly, I do," Jake said with an eager nod.

Adel felt a smile tickle her lips then, too.

"Then I give you the blessing of Abraham and Sarah, Isaac and Rebecca, Jacob and Rachel... May *Gott* richly bless your union."

Jake reached out and caught her hand and Adel smiled into her husband's eyes. Married... She was a wife again, and this time she was starting out with more than hopes for her future. She was starting out with a love so powerful that it left her weak in the knees. It didn't erase her past, or undo all the work and growth. It didn't take away from all that her marriage with Mark had given her. But it was a step forward with Jake at her side. Life was not over... Love was not a thing of the past.

Adel accepted the hugs and good wishes of the people present, and when they moved off toward the kitchen, Jake bent down and snuck in a kiss—the first kiss of their married life together.

"I love you," he whispered.

"I love you, too," she whispered back.

She may very well be the very worst matchmaker in all of Pennsylvania, but she'd make up for that in the coming months. Redemption would be bustling with weddings for the women who deserved the kind of love that she'd found.

Adel was already looking forward to going home that night, and sharing more kisses, more wedding cake and that quiet time at night when all they would hear would be their whispered hopes for the future...

* * * * *

If you enjoyed this story, be sure to pick up these previous books in Patricia Johns's Redemption's Amish Legacies series:

The Nanny's Amish Family
A Precious Christmas Gift
Wife on His Doorstep
Snowbound with the Amish Bachelor
Blended Amish Blessings

Available now from Love Inspired.

Dear Reader,

I had so much fun writing this story about a serious matchmaker and her handsome client! I hope you enjoy reading the story as much as I enjoyed writing it.

If you're looking for more Amish stories from me, I do have more books in this *Redemption's Amish Legacies* miniseries, as well as other books in my backlist that I hope you'll check out! Come by my website for a complete list at patriciajohns.com.

You can also find me on Facebook, where I have regular giveaways with other authors that I think you'll enjoy. I hope you'll look me up, because I'd love to connect with you.

Patricia

Get 4 FREE REWARDS!

We'll send you 2 FREE Books plus 2 FREE Mystery Gifts.

FREE Value Over **$20**

Both the **Love Inspired®** and **Love Inspired® Suspense** series feature compelling novels filled with inspirational romance, faith, forgiveness, and hope.

Get 4 FREE REWARDS!

We'll send you 2 FREE Books plus 2 FREE Mystery Gifts.

FREE Value Over **$20**

Both the **Harlequin® Special Edition** and **Harlequin® Heartwarming™** series feature compelling novels filled with stories of love and strength where the bonds of friendship, family and community unite.

YES! Please send me 2 FREE novels from the Harlequin Special Edition or Harlequin Heartwarming series and my 2 FREE gifts (gifts are worth about $10 retail). After receiving them, if I don't wish to receive any more books, I can return the shipping statement marked "cancel." If I don't cancel, I will receive 6 brand-new Harlequin Special Edition books every month and be billed just $4.99 each in the U.S or $5.74 each in Canada, a savings of at least 17% off the cover price or 4 brand-new Harlequin Heartwarming Larger-Print books every month and be billed just $5.74 each in the U.S. or $6.24 each in Canada, a savings of at least 21% off the cover price. It's quite a bargain! Shipping and handling is just 50¢ per book in the U.S. and $1.25 per book in Canada.* I understand that accepting the 2 free books and gifts places me under no obligation to buy anything. I can always return a shipment and cancel at any time. The free books and gifts are mine to keep no matter what I decide.

Choose one: ☐ **Harlequin Special Edition**   ☐ **Harlequin Heartwarming**
(235/335 HDN GNMP)   **Larger-Print**
(161/361 HDN GNPZ)

Name (please print)

Address   Apt. #

City   State/Province   Zip/Postal Code

Email: Please check this box ☐ if you would like to receive newsletters and promotional emails from Harlequin Enterprises ULC and its affiliates. You can unsubscribe anytime.

Mail to the Harlequin Reader Service:
IN U.S.A.: P.O. Box 1341, Buffalo, NY 14240-8531
IN CANADA: P.O. Box 603, Fort Erie, Ontario L2A 5X3

Want to try 2 free books from another series! Call 1-800-873-8635 or visit www.ReaderService.com.

COUNTRY LEGACY COLLECTION

19 FREE BOOKS IN ALL!

EMMETT
Diana Palmer

COURTED BY THE COWBOY
Sasha Summers

THE RANCHER AND THE BABY
Marie Ferrarella

Cowboys, adventure and romance await you in this new collection! Enjoy superb reading all year long with books by bestselling authors like Diana Palmer, Sasha Summers and Marie Ferrarella!